D0484742

CLING

Copyright © 2016 by Jeff Menapace
Published by Mind Mess Press
All Rights Reserved

CLING

All rights reserved. Without limiting the rights under copyright above, no part of this publication may be reproduced, stored in or introduced into any retrieval system, or transmitted in any form or by any means (electronic, mechanical, photocopying, recording or otherwise) without the prior written permission of the copyright owner or the publisher of this book.

This book is a work of fiction. Names, characters, places, and incidents are a product of the author's imagination or are used fictitiously. Any resemblance to actual events, locales, or persons, living or dead, is coincidental.

CLING

jeff menapace | kim bravo

MIND  MESS
PRESS

2016

one

Sadie was one of the rare few who had a sound baffle on her motorhorse. Most wanted to be heard, loud and intimidating, as they tore endless circles of dust throughout the wastelands and their fringe towns—small minds demanding fear and respect through primitive means akin to shouting. Sadie had survived as long as she had by being the snake without a rattle, well on her way to the next town over once a small mind realized it'd been bitten.

That and she was a martyr.

She could use her gift to determine whether entering the tavern was worth her time, but her observational skills were sharp—no point in enduring the inevitable sickness that followed after utilizing her gift when her eyes could serve her nearly as well. And so she took inventory of transportation outside the tavern: three camels; one horse; six motorhorses. No roadships. But then she hadn't expected one. Not in a small town like this. Had there been a roadship, she might have skipped the tavern altogether without a second thought, the owner of such a high-maintenance vehicle a likely warlord who would find exploiting her gift all too tempting.

But no roadships. Good. On to the likely owners of these other modes of transportation.

The camels assuredly belonged to nomads. Wandering men or women from distant towns who were content to slog their way across the land, preferring the camel's benefits of attrition over speed. Most nomads were relatively poor—hence why the camel and its ability to cover great distances with little food and water suited them so—but they were known to be hoarders. Quite often they carried with them a priceless artifact scattered innocuously among the useless ones. Such an artifact could be won at a card game if one were to know the true value of such an item—which Sadie would when the time was right.

The solitary horse was a no-go, the owner most likely a local. Horses did not have the endurance of camels in such a climate and were good for short distances before care was needed. This meant a stable nearby. Here in this town, or at the least the next town over. Sadie did not make it a habit to steal from locals. Bounty hunters were rampant in border towns like this. A big old wanted poster with her face plastered everywhere would be almost as bad as entering a warlord's compound and declaring herself a martyr.

The owners of the six motorhorses were where she would find decent money. The majority probably gang members, answering to a warlord, but it didn't mean their decision-making wasn't swallowed up by weak wills and excess. Sex and booze and what have you. Sadie's goal was to take whatever they had before they had a chance to indulge those weak wills, and by the looks of a few of their vehicles, there might be more to be had than she'd expected; their chassis bore utilitarian aesthetics like her own, the guts of the machines on full display. That display was big tanks and big engines that needed big fuel. There *had* to be good money inside. Fuel was nearly second prize to Clear, the substance that fought Cling.

Sadie killed the engine and parked her vehicle in line with the other motorhorses. She unstrapped the satchel from her back, set it to the ground, and squatted to inspect her tires. Both seemed okay. The treads were a little worn. She glanced over at the other vehicles and their thin black tires with spiky treads suited for the terrain. Like hers. Except theirs were in better shape. Perhaps she'd persuade one of the owners to throw his on the table after she took all his money.

"Look after it for you, lady?"

Sadie stood upright, picked up her satchel and slung it over one shoulder. She studied the man in front of her. He was small and skinny. Toothless, sun-battered, one good eye. Alcohol and a life of vagrancy shortening his life faster than Cling ever could.

"You looking after all of these?" she said, waving a hand down the row of motorhorses.

"Some."

Sadie pulled her long brown hair into a ponytail. She felt the grease on her hands and pined for a shower. She doubted this place even had a tub, the sign above that read BOOZE/CARDS/FOOD/SEX in crude paint a less-than-subtle giveaway.

"What'd they give you?" she said, snapping the band around her ponytail and then wiping her hands on her pants.

"A tenner for each."

Sadie dug into her back pocket and showed the man a ten.

He smiled. So did Sadie. And then her smile dropped as she stuffed the bill back into her pocket. "What'd they give you?" she asked again.

Now the man's smile dropped. "Five," he eventually said after a comment under his breath about women.

"Okay." Sadie started going into her satchel.

"The money," the man said.

Sadie produced a pair of leg irons. "Sit," she said.

The man took a step back. "You crazy, lady? Just what the hell you expect to do with those?"

"I expect to put them on your ankles so you can't run off with my vehicle."

The man snorted and gestured to the row of motorhorses. "None of them told me to wear anything like that."

"I'm guessing they're all men with ties to people even a drunk like you wouldn't cross. Seeing as I'm a *woman* and all..." She went toward him with the leg irons.

The man took another step back, shaking his head. "I ain't puttin' those on, lady."

"You want my money, and you will. And you can stop that nonsense about any of them giving you a fiver. What'd they promise you? Dinner? Booze? You'll be lucky if you don't get your throat cut for expecting anything once their money runs out."

The man looked away, ashamed of her truth.

"My word's good," Sadie said. "You can put these on and take *my* fiver. Up to you."

The man stared at the leg irons. "You don't need to put them on, lady. I won't run."

Sadie pulled a blade from her satchel and gestured with it as she spoke. "You can put the irons on so you can't run, or I can cut your Achilles so you'll never run. Which one will it be?"

The man's one good eye flinched with surprise. "You're *crazy*, lady."

Sadie shrugged. "Don't take my money then. Someone else will watch my vehicle."

"*Fine*," the man grumbled.

Sadie put the blade away and started attaching the leg irons to the man, putting the key in her pocket when she was done. She patted the seat of her motorhorse. "Take good care of her."

"*The money*," the man said.

"When I'm ready to leave."

"Suppose you end up like them? Suppose you spend it all and leave me nuthin?"

Sadie started toward the tavern entrance. "I'm not here to get drunk or laid."

"Well then, suppose you *lose* it all?"

"I don't lose." She went inside.

two

Sadie stepped inside the tavern. It was exactly as she'd expected—a place that did not stray from the blatant sign out front. There was booze, there were cards, there was food, there was sex. Drunk men mumbled and carried on, the majority using the bar ledge as legs. Circular tables shrouded in smoke held rough men cursing and slamming their fists or shots of whiskey after each hand lost or won. A solitary waitress wondered about offering bowls of what was billed to be cricket mush, but that Sadie knew was roach. And women, ravaged by Cling and booze and their trade, slunk about in little else but their leathery skin, offering their wares. Men too, though Sadie only spotted one, a tall sinewy piece of meat, his manhood scarcely covered by a loincloth. A warlord's bitch.

"Whatcha need, girl?" the bartender asked. He looked maybe thirty-five. In a better town, a better life, he'd have about five good years left.

"Something to eat," Sadie said.

"We got cricket."

Sadie pursed her lips in contempt. "I look like a mole to you?"

The bartender shrugged. "Wouldn't know. Never seen one. They never come in here."

"Because they'd be cooked before they ever got through the door, genius."

The bartender frowned. "Could come in at night."

"And I might start burrowing during the day."

The bartender frowned again. "You got a point to make anytime soon, lady?"

"My point is I didn't choose to live up here so I could eat bugs like a damn mole." Then, louder than necessary: "*Especially roach.*"

The bartender made a sudden hush face and began patting the air in a bid to get Sadie to lower her voice. "I might able to get you something later," he said softly.

Sadie shook her head, annoyed. "Just pour me gin." The bartender did, and she gulped it in one toss. "What's the hottest table?" she asked.

The bartender pointed past her shoulder. Sadie's eyes followed and landed on a large circular table. All hard men. One with gang colors.

"They the ones you're hoarding the real food for?" she said.

The bartender looked away, his pride dented. "Whatever, lady."

Sadie stood and headed toward the table.

.   .   .

Sadie lost the first several hands on purpose. Every man at the table had appeared initially threatened by her presence, and she didn't want to exacerbate things before she could get her hooks in. She used her gift, but sparingly, and it certainly wasn't to win. It was to confirm tells. If she used it too fast and too often to win, as many a greedy martyr was known to do, she wouldn't be able to fight the immediate sickness to follow. Better she let it trickle into her blood like a slow flu than to suddenly turn a ghostly white and puke gin and bile clear across the table. She'd be as good as dead after that.

Sadie felt safe enough to start winning, on the tells alone, by the tenth hand, yet she kept to her two-one-two-one strategy at first—win two, lose one; win two, lose one…

When the pots started getting bigger, it was time to flat-out cheat. She wanted four or five good pots, and then it would be time to bolt before anyone got wise. The snake without a rattle. And yet an inexplicable hypocrisy likening her to the greedy martyr she eschewed kept a heavy hand on her shoulder, keeping her seated as the pots grew larger and more readily…as did her sickness.

"You feeling okay there, lady?" A big man across from her. A blue do-rag representing his gang color covered his head. Below that, white scars ran intersecting lines across his tanned face like some inept grid. His eyes, squints from a life of relentless sun coupled with a growing skepticism for the integrity of the woman across from him, were unflinching. "You're looking kinda pale to me. Kinda sickly all of a sudden."

"I'm fine," Sadie said. This would have to be the last hand. She had it won, but considered folding. She'd made enough. The pot was big—the biggest yet—but what good would it do her if this man got the drop on her? The other players too for that matter. And then the same inexplicable hypocrisy that'd been keeping her at the table with its heavy hand on her shoulder now found her tongue. "Call," she said.

Everyone else at the table was out. Just Sadie and the Blue member, the pot big enough to keep a man or woman going for a good month with real meat, clean water, clean lodging, and a few spoils for whatever tickled you.

Blue laid down his cards slowly and one at a time, his eyes never leaving Sadie as he did so, as if he knew he'd already lost, didn't care, and was more interested on studying the tiniest reveal on Sadie's face so that he might be justified in claiming her scalp.

He laid down three tens and a pair of fours. A good hand. A damn good hand. Except Sadie knew about it the moment it touched the man's thick fingers. And she'd used her gift to see what the dealer was keeping in the stack. And it had been worth staying in—the reason she now coolly laid down four eights and then drew blood on the inside of her cheek to keep from smirking.

Blue pounded his meaty fist on the table, kicked back his chair, and stood, finger pointed at Sadie. "*Cheating whore!*"

Every chair at the table except Sadie's scooted back. Blue's scarred face hinted he was no stranger to a knife. His gang colors suggested he might even have access to good bullets. Though the other players at the table had been cheated just as much as Blue, he had clearly stamped his claim on this fight. You didn't interfere in another man's fight.

"I didn't cheat you, sir," Sadie calmly said. "It's just been my day is all."

Blue placed both fists on the table and leaned forward. Sadie could smell his breath. It didn't help the growing sickness inside her. "Then why is it you look like you're ready to drop, lady? You come in here pretty as a rose. Now you're looking like something I'd mercy-kill. And that's saying a lot coming from a man who don't have no mercy." He spit on the floor. "You wouldn't happen to be a martyr now, would you, Mercy-kill?"

"You think I'd be foolish enough to come in here if I was? Play *cards*? I know what happens to martyrs around here," Sadie said.

Blue leaned in further. "I don't think you *do*, Mercy-kill. No martyr's stupid enough to walk through those doors knowing what'd be coming to 'em if they got found out."

"Well, there you go…" Sadie said, splaying a hand. "If I was a martyr, I would know—*for sure*—what would happen. If my future was as bleak as you say it might be, why the hell would I stop in and embrace it?"

"Maybe you're one of them greedy martyrs. Don't know when to quit."

The smelly lump had her there.

"I'm thinking maybe I don't cut your throat right here," he continued. "Maybe first I take back my money you *stole* from me. Then maybe I take you to see my general. Oh, he'd make good use of you, Mercy-kill."

Sadie's strength was fading. She used the last of her gift to see whether the man's comment about cutting her throat implied he had no gun, only a knife.

She strained, her nausea like a malevolent flu. She closed her eyes long enough to forgive a long blink, and saw it all on the screens of her lids.

No gun. Certainly no bullets.

Sadie had both.

Blue went on, an arrogant smirk now matching his stare. "…And I'm not just talking about making good use of those pretty looks. I'm talking about mining some quality Clear—using up that crazy gift of yours until you really *are* a shriveled up mercy-kill."

"Curse," Sadie said, casually reaching into the satchel on her lap.

"What'd you say?"

"It's a curse, not a gift."

Blue growled, pulled his knife and flipped the table with one hand.

Sadie remained seated, the pistol she'd casually pulled from her satchel now at her hip and pointed up at Blue. He spotted it, yet had less than a second to appreciate its bite before Sadie blew two holes in his chest.

She might have put one more in his head in case he was wearing iron, but she needed the four remaining bullets in case any of the other patrons got frisky. Fortunately, they did not; all hands were in the air, backing away from the scene. As for Blue, he was already slumped in the corner, mercifully expelling the last of his rancid breath. No head shot needed.

Sadie stood, gun at her side. She felt unsteady on her feet. The need to vomit was the need to breathe. She approached the bartender, swaying a little like someone keen to belly up to the bar so they might resume imbibing and start swaying a lot. She was deathly pale, her face drenched in sweat. Though she knew it wasn't necessary, she pointed the gun at the bartender, desperate to expedite everything so she could head outside and puke her guts out.

"Food," she said. "*Real* food."

The bartender quickly turned and opened a small cooler on the floor. He returned with a sizeable lump tied up in butcher paper. "It's camel," he said.

Sadie nodded, stuffed the meat into her satchel, and then gave him a fiver from her winnings.

"No charge," he said.

Sadie closed her eyes and exhaled through her nose, pleading with her nausea. "Don't make me a bigger bitch than I already am."

The bartender nodded and slid the fiver off the bar. "That man was with the Blue."

"I noticed."

"His people will come looking for you, especially if they hear you're a martyr."

"And how would they hear that?" Sadie turned to the crowd of patrons and raised her gun on them. All hands went in the air once again. "Anyone see anything here today?"

Some chose to drop their eyes to the floor, some chose adamant shakes of the head. One man kept his chin high, a scowl on his face. Sadie recognized him as a man who'd sat at the card table with her. Someone she'd cleaned out early in the game. He had every right to be as pissed off as he looked. Still…

"What about you, sir?" she said to the man. "You see anything here today?"

The man nodded and stepped forward, chin still high, chest out. "I surely did, martyr bitch."

Sadie shot the man between the eyes, dropping him stone dead. There were gasps and brief cries of fear. Sadie raised the gun on the group again. "Anyone else wanna force my hand?"

No takers this time.

Sadie turned back to the bar and placed a tenner on it. "For the mess."

The bartender took the money. "Geez, lady, just where on earth did you manage to find good bullets for a pistol?"

"I'm a martyr, dummy." She laid her pistol on the counter, index finger stroking the trigger. "Or am I?"

The bartender glanced down at the gun with only his eyes, then back up at Sadie. "No, ma'am, you're surely not."

Sadie nodded once, a look of self-contempt tugging at her face as she turned to leave. *So what the hell happened to the snake without the rattle, girl?*

.   .   .

Sadie exited the tavern and went right for her motorhorse. The man with the leg irons was waiting.

"Please tell me you got somethin' for me, lady."

Sadie turned and barfed. The man recoiled in disgust.

"You said you weren't drinkin'!"

Sadie straightened up and wiped her mouth. "I wasn't." She took the key from her pocket and removed the leg irons.

The man rubbed at his ankles. "Was it the food?"

"No." Sadie took a twenty from her satchel. She needed to hurry; her sickness was not over.

"I heard gunshots in there. What happened?"

"Don't know." She climbed onto her motorhorse. "Here."

The man took the money and looked at it in disbelief. "A *twenty*? Hot damn! You really don't lose, do you?"

Sadie started her motorhorse. "Ever hear the expression that cheaters never win?"

The man nodded, his face still one big grin from the twenty in his hand, the endless bottles of gin it could buy.

"Yeah, well, it's bullshit." Sadie gunned her engine and sped away, leaving the man in a wave of dust. He didn't seem to mind.

.   .   .

Sadie didn't make it far. If she'd kept going in her state, an accident would have been inevitable. She'd left the town twenty, maybe thirty miles behind—enough to pull to the side of the road and finish the needs the sickness demanded without bother.

And there *would* be bother. She wasn't stupid enough to think otherwise. Wasn't stupid *at all*. She had no death wish either. So why? Why dismiss your better judgment as easily as the bullet you put in that man's head? The two you put in the Blue's chest?

The Blue.

Oh, you fool. Yes, there would be bother. Somehow, someway, there would be—

Sadie dropped to her knees and retched. And then retched again. She rolled onto her side, fetal, hoping beyond hope someone didn't happen by. She'd be helpless to defend herself at this stage.

She rolled onto her back, too weak to lift a hand to her brow and shield herself from the brutal sun. *You've no one to blame but yourself. You stayed too long, used too much. Why?* Amidst the constant nausea, her fading consciousness, the same word over and over like the prodding query of a persistent child: *Why?*

Too many martyrs were greedy fools, using their gift too often, having the resulting sickness claim their lives far too prematurely before Cling ever could.

Too many martyrs were careless in hiding their identities, allowing themselves to be snatched up by a warlord, their gift exploited as they were forced to roam the wastelands, locating pockets of Clear until their bodies were empty shells, the sickness claiming them without prejudice, just as it had done the greedy.

But not Sadie. She was neither greedy, nor careless. Until today. She'd made it to thirty-five relatively unscathed. An admirable feat for a rogue. A continued life of subtlety might just see her reach the life expectancy of forty—even beyond if she ever decided to mine Clear for the purposes of extending her life expectancy as opposed to eradicating the damages done to her body by utilizing her gift. It was a game of balance, one that Sadie was well-versed in. One step forward, one step back. There was always the hope that an immense pocket of Clear could be located through one session with her gift, enough to extend her life expectancy without ever having to get sick again, but such hopes were akin to those who believed a utopia was only "one town away." A prospect—increasingly delusional as each day bullied you into the next—that claimed Sadie as well.

And maybe that was it. The answer to *why?*

Maybe somewhere in a subconscious pocket of her hardened mind, she was giving up hope. Ready to declare her "gift" to the world and embrace the swift and inevitable fate to come at the hands of a warlord or a gun or even her own body, should she continue to adopt such a gluttonous use of her gift. Surely accepting one's unfortunate here-and-now was preferable to wandering on endlessly, taunted by hope.

It was not an epiphany, but it was enough of a realization to allow Sadie momentary peace of mind. She passed out.

three

Rafael Carrera Allende sat at his desk in the living room of the apartment he shared with his friend Teir, studying an old printed text on environmental toxicology. He had missed an important community health meeting two hours ago and knew his father and grandmother would be disappointed. Though only twenty years old, he was a prodigy and a polymath. Had long been a gifted healer and possessed an understanding of Cling and its elusive remedy that rivaled the understanding of the most senior healers in their community. He hoped his absence from the meeting would be forgiven.

Rafael stood from his desk to stretch and went into the bathroom to wash his hands and splash his face. The mirror above the basin reflected short dark hair, dark brown eyes, and light brown skin that always appeared sun-kissed despite his sunless subterranean life.

He was headed for the kitchen area to put on water for tea when he heard muffled sounds of distress coming from the bedroom down the hall, and he hurried in to kneel beside his friend's bed.

Though the room was shrouded in darkness, he could see well in the dim light from the hallway. An adolescent boy lay twisted in the blankets, thrashing and groaning. Rafael spoke Teir's name once, and then again.

Teir jolted awake and sat up, gasping for breath. "Rafa?"

"Right here."

"What time is it?" His voice was thick with panic.

"Just past twenty hours."

Teir ran a trembling hand through blond hair that reached his shoulders, pale blue eyes glistening. "I fell asleep."

"Yes."

"While you were reading to me."

"Yes."

Teir lifted the blanket and pressed it to his damp eyes, breath still coming in rapid, uneven gasps.

"Do you want some water?" Rafa asked.

"Yes, please," came the reply from behind the blanket.

Rafa retrieved the canteen from the kitchen, poured some water into a cup, and returned to sit on the bed beside his friend. Teir lowered the blanket and shoved a clump of hair behind his ear.

"Do you think you can hold the cup?" Rafa asked.

Teir lifted his hands, but they shook so violently that he let them drop into his lap.

Rafa placed a steadying hand on Teir's back and held the cup to his mouth. "Don't drink it too fast."

Teir slowly drained the cup, then sat staring into the darkness.

Rafa searched the boy's face, but it revealed nothing, his unseeing gaze blank. Gradually his breathing calmed.

"Are you hungry?" Rafa asked.

Teir shrugged, paused, then nodded. "Amaline and Ian are playing in D Caff at twenty-one hours."

Rafa managed a smile. "Would you like to go?"

"Would you?"

"Sure."

. . .

They both washed and dressed. Teir pulled on his black military boots, which had zippers as well as laces, and Rafa watched him easily zip them with his shaking hands. Rafa had given the boots to Teir for his fourteenth birthday the week before, and Teir had been terribly pleased to have sturdy shoes that did not require him to fumble with laces.

No one knew the boy's origin, his age was merely a guess, and Teir himself had no memory of his early life or even his given name, but his birthday was celebrated on the day he'd joined the community eight years ago. During an expedition above ground, Rafa had found him under a creosote bush, beaten, starved, and near death, wearing an iron collar and shackles. Rafa had saved his life and had taken care of him ever since.

"Izar offered to give you a haircut," Rafa said as he watched Teir pull his fingers through his unruly flaxen waves.

"Does it look bad?" Teir asked.

"Not at all. She just thought it might be easier for you without it hanging in your eyes. She also said, 'It hides his handsome face.' That's a direct quote."

Teir shook his head with a blushing smile. "I like it long."

"It suits you."

Though Rafa had named him for a character from Greek mythology who appeared in works by Homer and Sophocles, Teir much more resembled a young Norse god from the pages of the *Poetic Edda*. Rafa planned to read many of the great ancient texts to him someday. Teir's sharp mind delighted in academic learning, and Rafa enjoyed nothing more than indulging him. But although the ancient texts were works of unsurpassed excellence, their imagery and subject matter were often dark and difficult, harrowing material for anyone, especially for a boy who had known true evil at such a young age. Rafa knew he could no more shelter Teir from the harsh realities of life than he could recover his friend's lost childhood, but he strongly wished to avoid fueling his nightmares.

.   .   .

They left the apartment and headed toward the cafe. Teir walked beside Rafa, keeping the fingertips of one hand in contact with the wall as they moved. Rafa had determined years ago, after pouring over the extant medical literature in the community's library, that Teir's poor vision and hand tremors were genetic traits and not the results of abuse or disease. His vision had neither worsened nor improved in eight years, and he had adapted remarkably well. His low visual acuity and lack of central vision made him functionally blind, and he had no color perception, but his peripheral vision and other senses allowed him spatial orientation and independent mobility. For the past two years, one of his favorite activities while Rafa was immersed in his work had been solo exploration of the sprawling network of halls, chambers and tunnels that comprised their world, and his mind now contained a detailed map of every inch of public space.

The cavernous structure that housed their community had been built, equipped, and furnished by the wealthy survivalists who sheltered in its depths from the cataclysm that caused the Event. Many of these inhabitants had stayed for less than a generation before returning to the surface, secure in their belief that it was once again safe and preferable to life underground. Thereafter, the present community began to take root: judicious leaders guided by prescient academics who had come to realize that the crisis humanity faced was far from over and that long-term survival would require deprivation and sacrifice.

Rafa counted several of the community's founders in his lineage, but their people were expressly welcoming to peaceful newcomers who shared their broad-minded values, and the structure currently housed nearly four hundred people. The accommodations were no longer luxurious, now substantially worse for the wear, and an immense amount of work was required to keep everything running smoothly, both mechanically and socially, but every one of its inhabitants believed it was worth the effort to keep them safe from the chaos and sickness above.

Though it was becoming clearer with each passing day that they were no longer as safe from the sickness as they had once been.

Rafa noticed the LED lighting at their feet, the hallway's only illumination, was dimmer than usual. That meant they'd recently had a few days of bad weather. Heavy cloud cover and no wind prevented the solar panels and wind turbines from doing their jobs, so all the stored power was in ration mode to keep essential functions running—agriculture; food preparation and storage; air, water and waste purification. Too many more bad weather days would have them completely in the dark for a while.

"You wanna stop at the library?" Teir asked.

"Not now. They're getting ready to close, and you're hungry. Maybe tomorrow evening. Dilys finished setting up the audiobike in the youth lounge."

Teir laughed quietly. "You really want me to use that thing."

"It's an ideal educational and fitness device for you," Rafa told him. "And Dilys is very proud of it. She'll be pleased to see you using it."

The unit was a beloved brainchild of the community's machinist-turned-innovator. It was an audiobook device powered by a battery that was charged by a stationary bicycle. Rafa imagined Teir wearing himself out listening to a professional narration of Rudyard Kipling's *Kim* and then taking a nap filled with dreams of fantastic adventures in nineteenth-century India.

"I like it when *you* read to me," Teir said.

"And as long as there's breath in me I will, but unless you've developed a sudden interest in astrobiology and evolutionary genetics, I'm afraid the books I most urgently need to read might bore you."

"Rafael!" a voice called behind them. They both stopped and turned, and Rafa's gut clenched at the sight of Julen approaching. "Where were you at eighteen hours?" his father asked.

"At home," Rafa said quietly.

Julen frowned. "Why weren't you at the meeting in North Hall?"

Rafa searched his conscience for an acceptable response. "I—" The man's dark eyes bore into him. "I couldn't—"

Julen stepped closer to him, not threatening, merely intense, as was his way. "You know how important these meetings are. The health of our community is at stake. How could you fail to attend?"

Julen Carrera was a great man. Honest and fair and brave, a respected organizer, and at the age of forty well on his way to becoming a revered elder. He was proud of his son's prodigious intelligence but had always struggled to understand Rafa's motivations and behavior, always relying on his late wife to provide insight and wisdom in matters regarding their son. To Rafa, this truth was suddenly never truer, and his boundless grief for his mother flared in its gilded box. Nine years later, his pain was still as raw as the day she died. It struck him speechless.

Then Teir spoke. "It's my fault. He passed out at his desk. He asked me to wake him if he fell asleep, and I forgot."

Julen fixed the boy with a gaze that Rafa was glad Teir couldn't see. Not contempt or irritation. Pity. He looked again at Rafa. "You were missed, son. Your input is invaluable, as you well know. Next time, set an alarm."

"Yes, sir."

"Elixa will brief you tomorrow."

Rafa nodded, suddenly anxious that he would have to lie to his grandmother to preserve Teir's cover. And she would know it was a lie. She would also know that Teir was the reason for Rafa's absence. Fortunately she was extremely fond of her grandson and his young friend.

Julen dismissed them, and they continued the rest of the way in silence.

four

They reached the cafe and stepped inside. The show hadn't yet started, but the main room, large and circular with a stage at its center, was already crowded and loud. Teir pressed close to Rafa and gripped his arm firmly, and Rafa led him toward a small table against the wall.

"Why'd you miss the meeting?" Teir asked.

"I didn't want to leave you while you were sleeping."

"You should have woken me up."

"You need your rest," Rafa said. "Sleep is very important for healthy brain development in adolescents, and the quality of yours has been compromised lately."

"You not missing meetings is important too."

Rafa steered him to the table. "You're right, and so am I. The end. What do you want to eat?"

"Cricket bars." Teir sat down in one of the chairs.

"Okay. How about some jumil paste on them?"

"Why do you always want me to eat jumiles?" Teir asked with a grimace. "They're bitter."

"They're extremely nutritious, and they help you relax. I've been feeding them to you for years and hiding the taste with more flavorful ingredients."

"Then why stop deceiving me if that's worked so far?"

"I'd prefer if you ate them by choice simply because they're good for you."

Teir rolled his pale eyes in mock disgust. "Fine. Ruin my tasty cricket bars with jumil paste."

"I'll have them only put it on one bar."

"Thanks."

Rafa made his way to the counter, placed their order and returned with their meal.

"What'd you get?" Teir asked after a few bites of a jumil-smeared cricket bar.

Rafa watched the boy's hand tremble as he fed himself. The tremors combined with his tenacity granted him an unusual grace.

"Bamboo worms, palm grubs, and locust," Rafa said. "Do you want some?"

Teir smiled and nodded. Rafa fed him a mouthful and wondered whether there would ever come a time when Teir's appetite ceased to please him. The boy had been emaciated when Rafa found him, and so weak he'd been unable to feed himself for months. His survival had been nothing short of a miracle; every pound he'd gained in the past eight years, a triumph. Now he was an image of robust health. Rafa was not a small man, and Teir was already as broad-shouldered as him and nearly as tall. By his next birthday, he would be bigger than Rafa. Full grown, he would be one of the largest men in the community.

"More?" Rafa asked.

Teir nodded again, and Rafa obliged.

"You ever had animal meat?" Teir asked after he'd chewed and swallowed.

"Once, when I was young. Elixa and my parents brought me and Izar to a celebration held by a group of nomads who'd become very friendly with our community."

"What kind of animal?"

"Chicken."

"What did it taste like?"

Rafa thought back to the experience. "Like nothing I've ever eaten."

"Did you like it?"

"It was all right. I wouldn't go out of my way to eat it again."

"How come?"

"The animals were ritually slaughtered and butchered as part of the celebration. All the blood was nauseating."

Teir frowned. "You're a healer. You see blood all the time."

"And I've never had the urge to eat a patient."

Teir laughed and took another bite of his cricket bar.

"Hello, little brothers."

Rafa looked up to see his sister, Izar, accompanied by a woman with long red hair.

"Mind if we join you?" Izar asked.

"Not at all." He motioned to the empty chairs at the table.

The women sat, and Izar turned to her companion. "Sirena, this is my brother, Rafael, and our friend Teir."

"Rafa," he said as he extended his hand to Sirena. Her smile was warm, her grip firm. Rafa nudged Teir gently, and he took the cue to extend his hand to shake Sirena's.

"So why weren't you at the meeting?" Izar asked.

Rafa's anxiety sparked at the thought of lying to his sister.

Again Teir rescued him. "He fell asleep, and I forgot to wake him."

Izar limited her response to a skeptical glare at Teir, then at her brother, apparently unwilling to challenge the validity of such an unlikely excuse in front of Sirena.

"They're moving ahead with the plan to make contact with the tribes beyond the plateau about locating a martyr," Izar said.

Rafa made no effort to disguise his shock. "Why? I thought we all agreed to hold off for a few more weeks."

"Well, tonight it was brought up and voted on again, and the motion passed. If you hadn't been *asleep*, you could have restated your case and cast your vote."

Teir slapped an open palm on the tabletop, and several heads turned in his direction. "Everybody says how smart he is and asks for his advice, and then they don't take it!"

"I happen to agree with that," Izar said. "But since last week's meeting, three more people have fallen ill." She hesitated. "And not all of the victims are elders. Two are in their forties."

A chill shot up Rafa's spine.

"So it's been decided," Izar continued. "We leave in two days." She nodded to Sirena beside her. "This gifted lady will be our translator."

"How many languages do you know?" Rafa asked Sirena, trying to distract himself from his dread with polite conversation.

"Seven fluently," she told him. "And I can make basic conversation in several more." Her voice carried the hint of an accent.

"Impressive." He hoped he sounded sincere. He truly was impressed. He himself knew only five languages, two of which were dead and one which was critically endangered. "How did you learn them?"

"I was raised a nomad. My parents knew many languages and taught me, and I learned more in our travels."

He could see in the dim light that her nose and cheeks were sprinkled generously with freckles, evidence of years spent under the sun, though she had clearly managed to care for herself despite the harsh conditions of a nomadic life above ground. He guessed her age to be a year or two older than Izar, twenty-five perhaps.

"How did you come to be with us?" he asked.

"My parents had long known of the kindness of your people and your willingness to take in outsiders." Her smile was sad, but her voice remained steady. "They brought me here last year, a month before the sickness claimed them both. I was their only child."

"I'm very sorry," Rafa said, too quietly to be heard above the noise of the crowd. She nonetheless received his sentiment with a grateful nod.

Her gaze lifted to something behind him, her smile brightened, and she waved coyly, then turned back to him and Teir. "I must run. It was a pleasure meeting you both." She turned to Izar, whispered something; they laughed conspiratorially, then Sirena kissed Izar's cheek and disappeared into the crowd as Amaline and Ian entered the room to clamorous applause. Ian sat at his drums and Amaline at her piano, and without delay the duo launched into their set. Rafa marveled that two people could make so much glorious noise.

Teir had finished his cricket bars, and Rafa pushed his own half-eaten meal in front of the boy, who shook his head.

Rafa guessed the cause of his refusal was due in part to the futility of trying to eat with a utensil while his tremors were so severe. "Eat it with your fingers."

"You sure?" Teir asked.

"Are you concerned about offending onlookers with poor manners?"

Teir grinned. "No. I just don't wanna eat your food."

"I ate earlier. I got this for you."

Teir's grin widened, and his objections halted. It lifted Rafa's spirits to watch him empty the bowl as his blond head bobbed with the music.

Rafa, Teir, and Izar sat quietly for a while, enjoying the show. A reverent hush had fallen over the crowd, conversation having ceased as much out of respect for the artists as the impracticality of trying to be heard above the delightful racket.

"I need to borrow your bestie for a few minutes, Teiresias," Izar said during a pause between songs. "Will you be all right by yourself?"

"What if I said no?" Teir replied with a smirk.

She reached out and cupped his chin affectionately. "I would tell you that I'm borrowing him anyway and I only asked to be polite."

Teir narrowed his eyes, feigning irritation, and motioned her and Rafa away with a few regal flicks of his hand. Rafa laughed quietly, stood, and followed his sister through the crowd.

. . .

In addition to having a husband and child, Izar was the community's full-time physical therapist. Rafa of course had his own work and cared for Teir. This meant brother and sister had had no time alone together for several weeks, and Rafa was eager to speak with Izar about Teir's nightmares. Perhaps she sensed his need. Aside from Teir and his grandmother Elixa, Izar was his closest friend.

Rafa followed his sister out of the cafe and several paces down the hall to a small alcove with a curved bench seat and checkerboard table. He sat down beside her, and she turned to him.

"How is he?" she asked. "He looks exhausted."

"He's worse," Rafa said. "Every time he falls asleep, he wakes in a full-blown panic a few hours later."

Concern bloomed across Izar's face. "Which is why you look exhausted too. Has he told you what the dreams are about?"

Rafa shook his head. "He still doesn't remember them."

"What have you been reading to him lately?" she asked.

"You *know* I'm very careful about what I read to him."

"Are you able to wake him during a dream?"

"Usually. Sometimes it's difficult without touching him." Rafa had borne bruises around his neck for a week the last time he'd touched Teir while the boy was in the throes of a nightmare.

"Have you spoken to Elixa?" she asked.

"He doesn't want me to."

"Why?"

"He doesn't want to worry her."

Izar's dark eyes shimmered with benevolence. "I think you should speak to her anyway. He may be advanced for his age, but he is still a child and doesn't always know what's best for him." She paused, clearly conflicted with how to proceed. "Which brings me to why I needed to speak with you." There was an ominous note of regret in her words. "He has completely lost interest in his strength and agility exercises. All he wants now is combat training, and I just—I need a break from working with him. He's been fully recovered and self-sufficient for a long time now. He no longer needs my help."

Rafa's mood plummeted. Teir relished any opportunity to develop his natural talents for combat and had gained so much from the training he'd acquired under Izar's skillful guidance. None of the other combat-trained community members were willing to work with Teir due to their discomfort with what they perceived as his limitations. Fortunately, Izar was twice the warrior of all her peers. As children, while Rafa had busied himself with books and the healing arts, she'd learned to defend her home and loved ones with formidable intensity. For a while, she had delighted in passing that knowledge on to Teir, who had proved himself an exceptional student by any standards.

"But he *does* need your help," Rafa said. "The only time he gets a good night's sleep is after a session with you; his tremors all but vanish when he's well-rested." He knew she was aware of all this, but his desperation forced him to say it. He dreaded the thought of taking this away from Teir. There was precious little in their austere world to give him the sense of duty and purpose he craved.

"And I'm thrilled that it's helped. You know I could not possibly care more for him if he was our own blood. He is as much my brother as you are. But he's become so *intense*. He's a skilled opponent, and I'm terribly proud of him, but I find myself using increasing force in our sessions. If I keep working with him, I'm afraid he'll get hurt."

A rare flash of anger surged through Rafa. "He is not *fragile*. You of all people should know that. He is stronger and healthier than most boys his age. He just needs to learn control."

"I'm sorry, Rafa; I've made my decision. I would appreciate your respect." Her tone had an edge that warned him to push no further.

A long silence passed between them.

"Please speak to Elixa about his dreams," she said finally, her voice once again infused with its maternal tenderness. "You're doing an extraordinary job helping him become an intelligent and mature adult. He is more self-possessed than those twice his age who haven't known a fraction of the trauma he has. But you don't have to do it all on your own. You may be smarter than all of us, but you're still barely an adult yourself, and you play a critical role in our community." She shook her head, smiling sadly. "Mama would be so proud of you." Then she kissed his cheek. "Tell Teir I said goodnight."

He sat and watched her silhouette as she disappeared down the long dim hallway, and he remained seated, drifting in memories for a long time.

.   .   .

In the cafe, Teir was slumped in his seat, head forward, hair in his face, moving gently to the rhythm of a rousing and infectious song. The song ended, and the audience erupted in vigorous approval. Amaline thanked the audience, and the duo left the stage.

Teir lifted his head, pushed his hair from his eyes, and smiled.

Rafa placed a hand on his shoulder, leaned over, and spoke into his ear to be heard above the crowd. "Let's go. I'll read you some more of *Around the World in Eighty Days*, and we'll see how Phileas Fogg manages with the elephant."

Teir squinted as he rose from his seat. "Elephant?" Then recollection dawned. "Oh, yeah. They need to catch a boat in Calcutta to get to Hong Kong, but the train tracks weren't finished, so he bought an elephant." He stepped to Rafa's side and slipped a hand around his friend's arm.

They left the cafe and made their way home.

five

Finn entered the tavern and headed directly for the bar. Some tables fell silent and gaped as he passed; some whispered nervously to one another. Many of the bolder patrons fingered their weapons beneath their tables, ready to claim such an infamous scalp should the opportunity present itself, though technically there wouldn't be much of a scalp to claim—Finn's head was shaved and, like his face, was heavily tanned with only a faint dusting of stubble.

"Finn, right?" the bartender asked as soon as Finn settled onto his stool. "Heard you might be passing through."

"*Good* whiskey," Finn said without pleasantries. He was too damn tired after a day of traveling for pleasantries. Besides, fools often mistook kindness for weakness. He was in no mood to deal with fools.

The bartender—a rail-thin bespectacled man with a brown derby sitting atop a head of long, greasy black hair—nodded, squatted, and disappeared behind the bar for a moment, and then reappeared with a bottle that he placed in front of Finn. "Best I got," the bartender said as he slid a shot glass next to the bottle.

Finn poured his first drink, brought it to his lips—

"And so then what the hell am I drinking over here?" a man to Finn's left broke in. The man was imbibing heavily, well on his way to being legless, but he was not a drunk. Drunks were meek, grateful if you even breathed on them after you'd had a drink. Though Finn spotted no gang colors on the man, it was obvious he wasn't meek, and not just from the transient courage booze provided.

"That's whiskey you got, mister," the bartender said. "Don't you worry."

The man was all mustache and eyebrows, and when he frowned, they seemed to touch and take up his whole face. "Well, then how come you didn't reach under the bar and pull me out a 'good' bottle when I come in? *I* want a 'good' bottle."

"You're drunk, ain't ya?" the bartender said. "Seems like the whiskey you've been drinking is doing its job just fine."

The man leaned into the bar. "I want some of what he's drinking, dammit. I want the *good* whiskey." Extra-heavy mockery on "good" this time.

The bartender threw a thumb toward Finn, who'd since resumed his drinking. "Well, that there's my only bottle. You can take it up with him if you want, but if I was you, I'd leave him be."

Finn, listening but looking straight ahead the entire time, enjoying his whiskey, knew what was going to happen next just as sure as the spider knows the fly.

"*Hey*," the man said to Finn. "Hey, you…fella. How about you share some of that with me?"

Finn glanced over at the man and actually managed a smile; his face would be sore tomorrow. "What's that?" Finn said.

The man pointed to the bottle in front of Finn. "Bartender says that's *good* whiskey. Better than what I got. I want me some of it."

Finn envisioned giving the man what he wanted by inserting the bottle into the first available orifice. But to waste good whiskey was a sin. And he was trying to lay low today, after all. Business to attend to.

"Tell you what," Finn began. "I'll make you a bet."

The man said nothing. Finn went on.

"I'm gonna bet you that I can drink this shot of whiskey…" Finn poured a fresh shot. He then leaned forward and snatched the bartender's derby off his head, only to place it over the shot glass, covering the drink completely. He then gestured towards the derby. "…Without ever touching that hat."

Mustache and eyebrows were one again. He snorted in disbelief. "You're saying you can drink *that* shot"—he pointed to the derby covering the drink—"without *ever* touching the hat?"

"That's right," Finn said.

The man snorted again. "What do you bet?"

Finn splayed a hand. "The whiskey, of course. The whole bottle. It's yours if I can't. But if I *can*, all I ask is that you leave."

"That's it? Just leave?"

"That's it."

"You're a fool, mister."

Finn shrugged. "You ready?"

"Don't you touch that hat," the man warned.

"Don't need to—" Finn gave a satisfied gasp and pretended to wipe his mouth. "It's already gone."

"Like hell it is!" The man snatched the derby. The shot of whiskey was still there. "*HA!*" the man said.

Finn casually picked up the shot and drank it. He then gestured to the derby in the man's grip. "Never touched it. Now leave."

The bartender started laughing. Onlookers who'd gathered to witness the incredulous wager began to laugh too. The man growled and lunged at Finn. Finn side-stepped the charge effortlessly and stuck out his foot. The man tripped over it and pitched forward, sprawling face-first onto the wooden floor. Finn was behind him instantly, turning him over with his boot and then pressing it hard into the man's neck, pinning him there. The man gurgled and flailed helplessly.

"On any other day, the flies would be grateful for the meal I just gave them." Finn pulled a knife and brandished it. "Though it sickens me to stoop to this, please ask around about me—know that what I'm telling you is true, and know how very, *very* lucky you were on this day." Finn slowly removed his boot from the man's throat but did not sheath his knife.

Finn's words, or perhaps such sound defeat both physically and mentally, were enough to start a rapid nod from the man as he quickly rolled onto all fours and scurried out the door amid another chorus of laughter.

Some people offered to buy Finn a drink afterwards, but he declined them all, each refusal with less good grace than the last. He wanted to sit in peace and drink his good whiskey—and wait.

. . .

They showed just before sunset. Finn spotted them as he was taking a leak outside by the side of the tavern. He never pissed indoors if he could help it. Too vulnerable.

The two men pulled up to the tavern on their motorhorses, and Finn immediately knew something was off. They were members of the Blue, yet their colors were subtly worn, a bandana wrapped around one boot on each; that was all. And the way they arrived at the tavern, killing their engines the second they rolled to a stop. Gang members were primal fools, preferred to roar and hoot their arrival for all to notice. These two members of the Blue who had asked for a meeting with Finn clearly didn't want to draw attention to themselves. And that was just fine by Finn. Fewer witnesses.

Finn strolled across the wooden porch of the tavern and greeted the two men as they were dusting themselves off from their ride. The sunset lighting was orange and pleasant; squinting wasn't mandatory. Both were tall and thin, one with long black hair and a heavy beard, the other bald with a dark blond goatee.

"Boys," Finn said.

"You Finn?" Beard asked.

"That's right. What's up?"

The cryptic reasons for their meeting had not snuffed the two gang members' swagger entirely. "Like to go inside and get us some whiskey before we go any further. That okay with you?" Bald said.

Finn stepped aside and waved a hand toward the tavern entrance. "Of course."

. . .

All three men approached the bar. Finn gestured to his bottle of whiskey, a third of it now gone. "Put that shit away," he said to the bartender. "Get us a good bottle."

The bartender gave a subtle smirk, tucked Finn's good whiskey behind the bar, and returned with the typical house bottle and three glasses. Beard poured immediately, he and Bald taking three shots in succession before Finn stomached his first; if it wasn't camel piss and gasoline, then Finn was a warlord's wench.

"Out with it then," Finn said once they'd settled at a table. "I'd like to be on the road before dark."

Bald and Beard leaned in; Finn did not. "No doubt a man in your line of work has heard about recent events?" Beard asked.

"I hear a lot," Finn said. "Be more specific."

Beard looked annoyed. "Events as it relates to *us*—our colors."

"You mean one of yours getting gunned down by a woman in broad daylight."

If Beard looked annoyed before, he was practically seething now. "Cold-blooded murder is what it was. Came up from behind and shot him while he was drinking. Stood no chance."

Finn leaned back in his chair. "I heard it differently."

Beard took his next drink straight from the bottle, swallowing down his rage.

Bald took over. "Doesn't matter how you heard it," he said, "one of ours is dead at her hand."

"All right," Finn said with a little shrug. "So…what? You need me to see to your revenge or something?"

"*Hell* no," Bald said. "We *will* see to that ourselves when the time comes. It's just that word is this one…apparently she's one of them martyr freaks."

Finn's eyebrows went up. "A martyr, huh? They're not the type to go advertising their identity. What makes you so sure?"

"Word around," Beard broke in.

"And word around is always reliable," Finn said with no attempt to hide his cheek.

"We know your reputation, Finn, but even you're not crazy enough to take on the Blue. So you can knock off all that clever talk of yours now, unless you want a ten-foot stake driven up your ass and spiked out in front of our compound for all to see."

Finn shrugged, beginning to look bored. "You boys came to me."

Now Bald grabbed the bottle and drank from it. "We come to you to help us track the martyr. No one's seen her since that day."

"She's probably in hiding. Best thing to do would be to wait it out. Once it all dies down and she thinks it's safe again, she'll show her face."

Bald and Beard said nothing, just took turns swigging from the bottle, clearly hiding something.

Finn smirked. "Let me guess; your general told you the same exact thing. Except you two thought if you went rogue and found her sooner than later—well, who knows what kind of praise he'd shower you with? And a *martyr*, no less. With the proper incentive, we're talking a living, breathing Clear detector, right? If that's not cause for a shot up the ranks for you two, then I don't know what is."

"There you go with that smart mouth again," Beard said.

"Yeah, smart as in correct. I am, aren't I?"

"So what if you are?" Bald said. "Our money's just as good as anyone else's. You want the job or not?"

"Sure," Finn said. "I'll need money upfront. Expenses."

"Where will you start?" Bald asked.

"I don't know," Finn said, plucking a fleck of grit off his jacket and casually flicking it away. "I'll think of something."

"Word is some moles got her," Bald said.

"Doubt that," Finn said.

"Why? Because it's the *word*?" Bald mocked.

"Let's just say that if moles did get her, it was to help, not hurt," Finn said.

"What are you, some kind of bug-eatin' mole-lover?" Bald said.

Beard barked out a laugh and clapped a hand on Bald's shoulder.

"Money upfront," Finn said again.

Beard shifted in his chair and reached for his back pocket.

"Not here," Finn said. "Around back." He slid back his chair and stood. "Stay and finish your bottle, just don't be all day about it. I'll be out back waiting."

.   .   .

Their drunken laughter announced their arrival before their presence did. They'd obviously finished the bottle as Finn had suggested, impairing them. Good. Though Finn had taken out multiple gang members at once, he'd be the first to admit he was no macho fool who was always eager to test his might. For Finn, the simplest way was always…the simplest. And these drunken idiots didn't get much simpler.

"Money," Finn said.

Beard looked east and west first.

"We're alone," Finn assured him.

Beard grunted and reached into his back pocket, producing a wad of dirty bills. "So how will this work?" he asked, handing the money over.

"First we seal the deal with a drink," Finn said, going into the satchel on his hip for a flask.

Beard and Bald's eyes lit up. Their pumps already primed, there could never be enough booze while they were still conscious.

Finn uncapped the flask, took his own swig, and handed it over. Beard snatched it first and gulped greedily. Bald then snatched it from his friend and did the same.

Finn spit his false swig out.

Both men said nothing, only stared at Finn with stunted expressions, alcohol dulling logic and reason.

"Can you boys count to ten?" Finn asked.

"Huh?" were Beard's last words before falling flat on his back, kicking up a sizeable outline of dust around him.

Bald managed no last words, pitching face-first into the ground instead.

Finn stepped towards Bald and, not wanting him to suffocate, rolled him over onto his back with his boot. Bald's eyes were open and blinking away the settling dust, yet they were the only part of his body that appeared able to move. His arms didn't work. Nor did his legs and voice. All but his eyes were paralyzed.

Finn approached Beard. His condition was identical to that of his fellow gang member's: a limp body with nothing but a pair of working eyes to convey fear.

Finn spit any remaining residue from his false swig. "That wasn't even close to ten seconds," he said with a chuckle. "Vidar told me it would be potent stuff."

The terror in Beard's eyes just then screamed louder than his voice ever could.

Vidar.

Finn smirked and said: "Oh yeah…he's got a special surprise waiting for you boys."

six

To many, the name Vidar was a myth. Unlike most warlords, whose demands for notoriety were insatiable, Vidar was one for stealth, conducting the majority of his business by proxy through his most trusted subjects. Even many of his most regular clients had never seen his face; indeed, these people too sometimes wondered whether Vidar actually existed, whether perhaps he was nothing more than a clever creation preying on men's superstition and fear of the unknown as a deterrent for conflict as opposed to brute force.

To those both fortunate and unfortunate enough to be in the know, Vidar was very real.

Never one keen on the terms "warlord" or "gang," Vidar referred to himself as a businessman, his people a militia—well-disciplined soldiers who adhered to strict rules of conduct. And unlike the majority of ostentatious warlord compounds that all but screamed their prowess on the surface, Vidar and his army resided deep in the earth, within a sizeable and heavily guarded military bunker constructed lifetimes ago. The bunker's location, like Vidar, shared a similar status: legend to most, very real to a few both fortunate and not.

Finn was one of the fortunate. A significant one. When he appeared at the first of many steel doors leading into the heart of the bunker, he was met with both respect and curiosity by the armed soldiers standing guard.

Respect for who he was, and curiosity for the two lame and terrified-looking men Finn was pushing around in a wheelbarrow.

"What do you got there, Finn?" one of the guards asked.

"Just fulfilling a contract for the man," Finn said.

The second guard's eyebrow went up. Vidar was not one to abduct with impunity, unless they were—

"Two members of the Blue," Finn said.

No more needed to be said. "Leave them here," guard one said. "I'll get some men to bring them through."

Finn nodded a thanks and made his way farther down the dank concrete halls of the bunker toward Vidar's lair. He was met by three more steel doors every few hundred feet, each with armed soldiers standing guard on the other side, each nodding their respects to Finn, yet some still insisting he provide them with the necessary passwords, no exceptions.

The final door leading into Vidar's lair was no different than the rest—and that was the point. To Vidar, anonymity was more powerful than the plethora of arms he routinely dealt across the wastelands. Most warlords would have painted their names in victims' blood on the door; staked severed heads on either side; insisted on five—*ten*—soldiers keeping guard outside.

This was just another door. No different than the many other steel offerings one would encounter as they made their way through the winding corridors of the bunker.

Finn rapped his knuckles on the steel surface, sending a faint echo down the corridor from where he'd just came. The cover to the rectangular peephole slid open. A hard pair of eyes fixed on Finn.

"That you, Finn?" the eyes said.

"Yup."

"Five horse second and nine."

Finn sighed and cursed under his breath. The only thing that did change as you traveled deeper into the belly of the bunker was the difficulty of the passwords for each door. They were ever-changing puzzles, ones that relied on spelling and mathematics; Vidar insisted on proficiency in these skills from all his people.

"Come on, man, you know it's me," Finn said.

"Five horse second and nine."

Finn sighed again. He knew math, and he knew how to spell. He was also extremely tired and, truth be told, a little buzzed from the good whiskey the bartender had given him, the bottle now nestled safely in his satchel. He sighed again, closed his eyes, and worked the puzzle:

Five horse second and nine. Five horse. Fifth letter in horse is *e*. *E* for eight? Except he'd said five horse *second*. Second number starting with the letter *e* would be eleven. Five horse second equals eleven. Five horse second and nine. Eleven and nine. Eleven and nine equals twenty.

"Twenty," Finn eventually said.

The rectangular peephole slid shut, the heavy metal bolts clanked, and the steel door slowly opened, four armed guards greeting Finn, the one who'd quizzed him—Finn recognized his eyes—stepping forward with his hand extended.

"No hard feelings?" the guard asked.

"No, I get it," Finn said, taking the guard's hand. "God help the next guy who knocks on that door who doesn't know math or spelling."

A voice, deep and unmistakable, filled the chamber. "I have no use for anyone who doesn't know math or spelling." Vidar stepped out of the shadows and into the light. A desire for anonymity seemed to contradict the man's appearance. At well over six feet, heavily muscled, with long blond hair and icy blue eyes, any living warlord would have killed a thousand times over for Vidar's stature.

"Then business must be bad—" Finn said, flicking his chin towards the concrete ceiling. "Lotsa idiots up there."

Vidar laughed and patted Finn on his shoulder with a powerful hand. "How are you, my friend?"

"I come bearing gifts," Finn said.

Vidar cocked his head. "Oh?"

Finn nodded. "Wrapped in your favorite color."

Vidar ran a hand through his long blond hair. "I see," he said with a thinly veiled eagerness. "And where are these gifts now?"

"I left them with your men at the first gate. They're bringing them."

"I see," Vidar said again, unable now to resist a smile. He then stepped aside and waved a hand deeper into the chamber where the unmistakable glow of candlelight cast flickering shadows on the tunnel walls ahead. "After you, my friend."

.　　.　　.

Finn had been in Vidar's lair several times before. It was a sizeable dwelling that was more utilitarian than ornate—fitting to Vidar's very character. One particular area in the corner of the room stood out as the only measure of effort given in decoration. It was a shrine. Four brass urns on a mantel, an abundance of candles and flowers and memorabilia intertwined and encircling all.

Finn approached the shrine now and paid his respects to each individual urn—to Vidar's family.

First the grandchildren, Brandr and Tyra. The boy Brandr just five, his sister Tyra three when taken by the Blue.

Next was daughter-in-law Runa, mother of Brandr and Tyra. Her body had been shipped back to Vidar in pieces.

Lastly was Sten, husband to Runa, father to Brandr and Tyra, and only son to Vidar. He had not been shipped to Vidar as his wife had been. Instead his body had been staked in the desert nearby for both attrition and every hungry mouth to claim.

Finn had very few friends. Sten had been one of them. He pulled his good bottle of whiskey from his satchel, uncapped it, and then poured a small swallow by the base of Sten's urn. He then took a swig himself and nodded at the urn.

"I miss that crazy bastard," Finn said, turning toward Vidar.

Vidar stepped forward and took the bottle from Finn, drank heartily, and then handed the bottle back to Finn. "Exactly as we'd thought, yes?"

Finn nodded. "You were right. Their general told them to wait, and two geniuses got the idea not to. Figured they'd hire a bounty hunter to find her sooner than later and earn their general's praise."

"Knew they'd come to you first," Vidar said.

"My good looks?"

Vidar smiled. "The elixir worked as expected, I imagine?"

"Like a bullet to the head," Finn said. "What the hell was it?"

Vidar only smiled again. "Something a trusted nomad mixed for me."

"*Trusted* nomad? There's two words you don't hear used together often."

"You saw the result," Vidar said.

"Very true."

"Witnesses?" Vidar asked.

"Not that I know of. I made sure they were both nice and liquored up by the time they stumbled out of the tavern. Any onlookers would chalk up me dragging their sorry asses around as one fella helping out a couple of drunks. Either way, I don't give a shit. I fear the Blue as much as I fear indigestion."

Vidar laughed again. "They have numbers, my friend. Numbers often triumph skill."

"And numbers led by stupidity is like guiding a herd over a mountain. What does the son of a bitch call himself now? Gash? General Gash?"

All traces of Vidar's exuberance vanished. A stone face on the body of a mountain, he said: "Yes—that's what he calls himself."

"Scary," Finn said with a roll of the eyes.

Vidar's stone expression remained. "And my gifts now?"

Finn glanced over his shoulder. The shadows of two guards were in the distance. "We good yet?" Finn called.

"All good," one of the shadows replied.

"Bring them in," Vidar called.

The sound of the wheelbarrow's squeaky wheel could be heard first. Then the shadow on the tunnel wall—a silhouette of a wheelbarrow with arms and legs dangling over the side. When they arrived, the two members of the Blue were exactly as Finn remembered. Frightened eyes in a mess of useless flesh.

Finn took a final swig of his whiskey and then gestured to Vidar to hold on for a moment. Vidar granted him his wish, and Finn unzipped his fly and urinated on both men. "This will be the best thing that happens to you today," Finn said to them.

Vidar's laughter returned.

seven

Teir swept Rafa's legs out from under him, and the two slammed down onto the mat together with Teir on top. He knew Rafa was trying his best, but even his perfect vision and the fifteen pounds he had on Teir did him no good. Rafa wasn't a fighter, and he never would be. Which was the number one reason Teir had to be. It was a bad joke that the only way he could practice now was to beat up on the person he most wanted to protect. He wasn't sure whether he was annoyed or embarrassed that Izar needed a break from working with him. All he knew was that Rafa seemed just as upset about it as he was, so Teir kept his thoughts to himself.

"You okay?" he asked Rafa.

"Sure."

"We should stop."

"I'm fine."

"Yeah right." Teir locked his hand around Rafa's wrist, rose to a squat, and pulled his friend to his feet.

"I am," Rafa said. "My wounded pride is my only injury. And that is sufficiently offset by how impressed I am with your strength and skill." He paused, then added: "You've come so far."

"Not far enough," Teir said. "Not even close."

"I'm sorry I'm not a better opponent."

Teir shook his head. Rafa was way too nice. It worried Teir almost as much as his friend's lack of combat skills. "You're really smart, and you can make sick people healthy. That's a lot more important than being able to fight."

"I think both are equally important," Rafa said. "Especially in this world of ours."

Teir thought Rafa might be saying that just to make him feel better. Even so, it worked.

"Whatever you say. I still think we should stop." He grabbed Rafa's arm and pulled him toward the gym showers. "Come on, let's get clean so Elixa doesn't tell us we smell like camels again."

.   .   .

"There are my two favorite young men," Elixa said as they entered her office in the clinic.

Elixa was the wise and loving grandmother from every story that Rafa had ever read to Teir about a wise and loving grandmother. She smelled great, her skin and clothes were soft, and her voice was like music. In fact, her voice was the first music Teir had ever heard. When he was little and still so weak he couldn't walk, she would sit by his bed and sing to him, ancient songs in an ancient language. He didn't remember much from those days, but he would never forget that.

Teir aimed his gaze at the ceiling, and the large blind spot in the center of his vision lifted so he could see her move toward him. She wrapped her arms around him, and he hugged her.

"My goodness, Teiresias, I see you nearly every day, and it's still a shock that you've grown up to be so handsome. Not that you weren't a beautiful child, but all children are beautiful before life catches up with them." She put a hand on his cheek, which was now warm from her compliment. He'd never seen his own face and probably never would, but he didn't mind hearing that it was handsome. "How are you?" she asked. "You look tired."

"I'm fine. Rafa and I were at the gym early this morning. He let me beat him up for an hour, so go easy on him today." He hoped she didn't question him more about looking tired. He really didn't want her to know about how bad his nightmares were getting. He didn't remember them, he didn't want to, and he didn't want Elixa to worry about him. She'd done enough of that when he was a kid.

Elixa greeted Rafa and harassed him for missing the meeting the night before but didn't make too much of it. Instead she started filling him in on work that needed to be done.

Teir wandered out of the office and into the clinic's intake area. It was empty and quiet now, but in half an hour the rest of the staff would arrive, and it would start to fill with patients. The clinic had been his home for five years after he joined the community. Things had been rough for a while. He'd spent his first month barely conscious, then a few more months tired and weak, then a few years confused and frustrated. At least he'd always felt safe. Rafa had lived with him and taken care of him, Elixa was always nearby, and Izar had visited every day.

"I have to prep for an appointment," Rafa said behind him. "What are your plans?"

Teir turned to face him. "The usual: lurking in the shadows, making people uncomfortable."

Rafa chuckled. "We're booked solid until fourteen hours, and I have work to do with Elixa and a few other colleagues after that. I may not be home until after eighteen hours."

Teir frowned. With his schedule so packed, Rafa would forget to eat lunch.

"What is it?" Rafa asked.

"You work too hard," Teir said.

"You've mentioned that on several occasions."

They never argued, but this was a sore spot. "It's bad enough you've been taking care of me since you were twelve—"

"No," Rafa cut him off. "There's nothing bad about that. Nothing at all."

Teir shook his head. This conversation always went in circles, and he wasn't in the mood. "I'll find stuff to do today."

"Our schedule is light tomorrow, and Sasho will be here," Rafa told him. "You can help him bundle the sage that just finished drying."

That cheered Teir up some. The pharmacy tech was a little crazy, but not in a bad way. The guy had an opinion about everything, he wasn't afraid to share it, and his delivery was pure entertainment. "Okay."

Teir got a promise from Elixa that she'd make sure Rafa ate lunch, then he said his goodbyes and left them to their work.

.   .   .

Teir's first stop was the ceramic studio. He worked on the wheel until his legs were cramped from spinning it and his arms and shoulders ached from making sure the clay didn't fly across the room. He liked the feeling of the clay sliding through his fingers and changing shape as it spun, but the results were always terrible. His tremors weren't to blame as much as sheer lack of skill. Fortunately he didn't care. It wasn't about the results.

"Do you want me to fire it for you?" the studio manager asked. "We should have enough fuel to light the kiln by next week."

Teir laughed. "No thanks, Chen. I'll put it in the scrap bucket on my way out."

His next stop was his favorite bug farm, but when he stepped into the big, humid chamber, he heard the laughter of kids over the click and hum of thousands of insects. A class visit in progress.

"Teir!" the farmer called.

"Hey, Fahima. Teaching the kids about the food chain?"

"Of course," she said. "I'll be finished shortly. I made a batch of cricket and sowbug cookies, and they're wonderful."

"I'll stop by later."

He ate an early lunch at home, then went back for a visit with Fahima, whose cookies were indeed wonderful. After that he went to the gym to charge his flashlights on the rowing machine, another Dilys contraption she called the "rowlight." He rowed until both lights were fully charged. It took over an hour, but at least the workout eased his tremors. He then made another stop at home to change out of his sweaty clothes and wash up.

Now, standing in front of the bathroom mirror and staring at the large blind spot that hid his reflection, he said: "Time for a little adventure, Teiresias."

.   .   .

The tunnel was something he'd discovered a while ago. It was in a remote part of the complex that was used for storing supplies, so there was rarely anyone near the entrance door. "N-6" was painted on the door in bold black letters so large that Teir could easily read them even in the dim lighting. The inside of the tunnel, once he got past all the boxes and piles of stuff stacked within, was round like a tube, and the walls were smooth concrete, about six feet wide with a grated metal floor. It was at the lowest level of the complex, deep below the surface, and the depth never changed; he'd never come across any ladders, stairs or ramps inside. It didn't even turn, just continued straight in one direction. Although it was now only used for storage, it seemed like it could have originally been made as a way to connect one community to another, except they didn't have any neighbors.

None that he knew of anyway.

Each time he went in, he went a little farther, but last time he still hadn't reached the end before his flashlight died and he had to turn around and head back in the pitch dark. He'd never asked anyone about the tunnel, though he was sure it was no secret. Rafa's people had lived in the complex for a few generations. Someone had to know it existed, and maybe even why, but Teir had never heard anyone talk about it, and he'd never asked, not even Rafa. It was far more exciting that way.

He wore gloves and kept the fingertips of one hand touching the wall as he moved along. He kept the beam of the flashlight on the ground, and with his gaze fixed on the blackness in front of him, he used the outer vision below his blind spot to judge where he was stepping. Every few dozen steps he would stop and listen, sniff the air, pull off one glove, and press his hand flat against the wall, first on one side then the other, to see whether there was any vibration or whether the texture or temperature changed. He never felt or heard anything unusual. In fact it became eerily quiet when he went far enough. No buzz of generators or purifiers. A muffled silence. The scent changed, but it was just the air getting stale from lack of ventilation.

He'd been traveling a while when his first flashlight started to die. He kept going until it went out completely, then stopped and did his check: no strange noises, smells, vibrations, textures, or temperature changes.

If he turned on his second flashlight and kept going forward, he would end up traveling back toward home, at least part of the way, in the pitch dark again. It was only a little unnerving; the lighting in the community was low to begin with, but add his vision to the mix and he was more or less in the dark most of the time anyway.

And he was so curious. It wasn't as if it could go on forever. How much farther could it really be to the end?

He turned on the second flashlight and kept going.

.　　.　　.

Teir wasn't sure how much farther he'd gone when he heard it.

He stopped and stood as still and quiet as possible. Sight was a distraction when tuning in to his other senses, so he shut off the flashlight.

There were no changes in the air quality or smell. It didn't move at all against his skin, so he was reasonably sure he was still alone in the tunnel.

He pulled off a glove and placed his hand flat on the wall. Was that a low vibration?

Then he heard it again: Music? Shouting? A machine?

He stood in the center of the tunnel facing in the direction he'd been going and stood still with his hands at his sides.

The sound was coming from above. What the hell *was* it?

He stood for a long time, listening. It varied in volume and tone, so it wasn't a machine, but it didn't vary enough to be music.

Voices. He couldn't tell how many or exactly how far above the tunnel they were, but they were either loud or close, otherwise he wouldn't have been able to hear them, he reasoned.

He listened until they went quiet. Then he turned the light on, pulled a piece of white chalk out of his pocket and made a big *X* on the wall.

He turned toward home and walked with even paces, counting his steps all the way back to the tunnel's door.

eight

She's screaming. They're hurting her again. They want him to watch, but he can't see what's happening. He can only hear her screaming. He wants to help her but doesn't know what to do. He is so small, and they are so big, and there are so many of them.

Something hits his face very hard, and he falls down. He is hit again and again, on his face, his back, his stomach. It hurts, but he doesn't cry. He hears them laughing as he is pulled across the floor by his hair, closer to her.

Then he hears a noise like someone chopping wood.

Her screaming changes, and he knows they have done something terrible to her again.

They are laughing and cheering, and the air is filled with the smell of cooking meat.

Then someone is calling for him. They're using the wrong name, but he knows they're calling for him. He knows the voice. It's someone who helps him. Someone who doesn't belong here. If he follows the voice, she'll stop screaming, and he'll be safe—

Teir woke suddenly and sat up, launched himself to his feet, stumbled, and started to fall. He felt someone grab him, and he swung, fist hitting flesh. The hands released him with a gasp of pain. Teir lost his balance and hit the living room floor, then rolled onto his side and curled, eyes and throat burning.

"Teir? Are you awake?"

Teir rubbed furiously at his eyes. He'd just punched Rafa.

"Rafa?"

"Yes, it's me."

"Are you okay?"

There was a pause, and then the sounds of Rafa collecting himself.

"Rafa? Did I hurt you?"

"No more than you did this morning at the gym."

He heard Rafa moving toward him, then felt a hand on his shoulder.

"Are *you* all right?" Rafa asked.

Teir definitely wasn't all right, but they both knew that. "I think so," he said, rubbing his elbow and then his knee.

Rafa helped Teir back to the couch and sat him down. He then took a seat next to him and turned on a lamp so he could have a look at his friend's knee and elbow.

"Only scraped," Rafa concluded.

They sat quietly for a few minutes as Teir caught his breath and let his racing heart slow. He knew Rafa was watching him.

"I still don't remember them," Teir said, answering the question he knew Rafa wanted to ask him after every dream. "I just know something terrible is happening, and I can't do anything about it."

Out of the corner of his eye, he saw Rafa nod his head.

"What time is it?" Teir asked. He vaguely remembered passing out on the couch around eighteen thirty, tired from his busy day and worried that Rafa wasn't home yet.

"Nineteen hours," Rafa said.

"When did you get home from work?"

"A few minutes ago. I'm sorry I was late."

"You get all your work done?" Teir asked.

Rafa hesitated, like he was going to say something else but changed his mind at the last minute. "We did. How about I make us some dinner?"

.　　.　　.

afa was quiet during dinner. Not that he was ever chatty. If he wasn't see-patients, speaking at a meeting, or interrogating a librarian about his latest research topic, he let everyone else do most of the talking. But when it was just the two of them hanging out, the conversation flowed.

Not tonight though.

They played cards after dinner. When Teir was a kid, Rafa had made him a special deck with raised markings and big print. He'd taught Teir dozens of games over the years, some that helped him learn math or memory or strategy skills, and some that were just for fun. When they played against each other, Rafa usually won, but Teir didn't care. Rafa was the smartest person in the community. Playing a game with him was like playing against a machine. The challenge was exciting, and Teir appreciated that Rafa didn't baby him like everyone else did. And of course the rare games that Teir won were *very* satisfying.

Tonight Teir won a few games in a row, but it wasn't satisfying at all. Rafa lost because he wasn't paying attention. Something was up.

Rafa read him some more of *Around the World in Eighty Days*. Years ago he'd made Teir a huge map with raised lines where the borders between countries had been before the Event had ravaged the planet. Now they stood together in front of the map on the wall, Teir's fingertips touching the western edge of what used to be their own country. Rafa had just shown him the route across the Pacific Ocean that Phileas Fogg and Passepartout took from Japan to San Francisco. Then he told Teir that both places, with their brilliant people and vibrant cultures, had been eaten by the ocean because of the Event.

It wasn't like Rafa to say something so depressing. He was serious and hardworking, but he was also easygoing and content in his quiet way. The only time he got sad was when he talked about his mother, which was rare.

Teir decided it was time to ask. "Are you upset because I hit you after my nightmare?"

"Of course not," Rafa said quickly. "Why would you think that?"

Teir shrugged. "Seems like something's on your mind. Is everything okay?"

Rafa's long pause answered the question better than words ever could. "We need to talk," he eventually said.

Teir felt like he'd been gutted. He almost wished he had been. It would have hurt less.

Rafa was being sent on the expedition beyond the plateau to search for a martyr, and Teir had to stay behind. Julen thought Teir would be too distracting to Rafa if he went along.

Too distracting. As if he was still the helpless little kid who couldn't feed himself and stumbled around bumping into walls.

But far worse than his humiliation was the fact that the expedition would last for several days. They were going to meet with people they'd heard of but never met. And they would have to shelter in caves during the day so they wouldn't be baked or blinded by the sun. The caves might have only one entrance and exit. They could be trapped by bandits or a gang, with only Izar and three others who were combat trained to defend them.

Rafa would be in danger, and Teir wouldn't be there to protect him.

.   .   .

That night Teir's dreams were the worst they'd ever been. Except this time he remembered one of them: A gang had taken Rafa, and they were torturing him, chopping him into pieces. Teir was there, but he couldn't do anything except listen to his best friend die.

When he woke to find Rafa alive and whole, slumped next to him on the living room couch fast asleep, his emotions got the best of him. He inched in close and fell back to sleep with his head on his friend's shoulder.

nine

Teir woke to the sounds of Rafa in the kitchen. They didn't say much to each other as they made breakfast and ate. Teir cleaned up while Rafa packed and gathered the things he would need for the expedition.

They arrived at the clinic at eleven hours. Teir helped bundle the sage, but even Sasho's comedy act couldn't lift his spirits. When the pharmacy tech commented on Teir's foul mood, Teir almost punched him, and Elixa had to have words with them both.

Just before thirteen hours, Teir decided he'd had enough of trying to pretend that he wasn't ready to explode. He left the clinic and went straight home.

He lay on his bed with his gaze aimed at the ceiling. The same scenes played over and over in his mind until he was sure he had no choice.

He got up and began to pack.

.   .   .

Rafa hugged Teir goodbye, picked up his bag, and left without a word. Teir stood with his back against the closed door, singing quietly to himself, a song that taught children to count to twenty in the old language Rafa's family spoke, a trick Elixa had taught him to calm himself. It was the only thing that stopped him from charging out into the hall, grabbing Julen by the throat, and screaming at him.

Once he had himself under control, he stood for a while with his ear pressed against the apartment door. If he didn't time this exactly right, he'd get caught, and Julen would have him detained if he figured out what Teir was up to.

When the hall was clear, he went into the bedroom; put on a pair of cargo pants, his boots, a long-sleeved shirt, a thick black hoodie, and gloves; then grabbed his bag from under his bed and left the apartment.

·   ·   ·

The long journey to the surface was clear and quiet. Teir forced himself to take the many stairs slowly; it would be pretty damn dumb to trip and fall before he even got outside.

He used the spare key Rafa kept in his desk at home to unlock the door, opened it a little bit and listened. He heard voices in the distance. One of them was Izar's. They were far enough away that Teir felt he could slip out undetected, and he closed and locked the door quietly behind him.

The night air hit him like a slap in the face. Not a painful slap. Just a sharp reminder of what existed in this part of the world. The part that was as lawless and deadly as it was beautiful.

He inhaled deeply. Cool fresh air. Sweet poison.

He'd been to the surface several times in the past few years with Rafa and Sasho. Brief nighttime trips lasting no more than an hour, enough time to gather plants and bugs that couldn't be farmed in artificial light. They'd never gone far or done anything exciting, but it had always left him longing for more. It shocked him every time how amazing it was to breathe unfiltered air, smell the desert, feel a breeze on his skin, hear the sounds of nature around him.

What a pity the world had gone to hell.

He shook off his trance and started walking in the direction he knew Rafa and Izar and the rest of the party had gone, toward the main road, and he caught their trail right before they reached it. He pulled up his hood to hide his hair and kept to the bushes in case any of them looked back. If he wasn't careful, they would easily see him in the bright moonlight and he didn't want that. Not yet. Not until they were too far from home to bring him back. No way was he going back without Rafa.

He moved as quickly as he could, his gaze up and straight ahead so he could scan the ground in front of him. It was a lot harder without a flashlight. The bushes weren't thick, but there were also small trees, rocks, and holes to avoid. The moon's light was brighter than the halls he traveled every day in the community, but he knew those halls like a rat in a maze in one of those old science experiments Rafa had told him about, and the floors of the halls weren't littered with random obstacles—finding his way now, alone in this unfamiliar place, was a different game altogether.

.   .   .

They'd been moving for close to an hour, and Teir had only stumbled a few times, twice on rocks and twice in shallow holes, but he hadn't fallen. He kept his ears trained on Izar's conversation with Sirena since Rafa and the others had barely spoken. The women were cheerful and laughed enough that it was easy to keep track of them. Teir just hoped he was the only one listening. Anyone could be crouching in a moonless shadow waiting to jump out and take whatever they wanted from his unsuspecting friends. Their lack of caution bothered him.

He began trying to distract himself from worrying about his friends by picking out different smells on the breeze and trying to identify them. He knew many; a few were barely familiar. He would quiz Elixa later.

Oh damn. Elixa.

She was going to be so worried about him when she found out he was gone. He'd been so stressed about Rafa being out here without him that he hadn't even stopped to think of anything else.

He was trying to figure out how he was going to apologize to Elixa when he smelled something. Something wrong. It hit him suddenly and he stopped walking. He wondered why his friends hadn't noticed it when they'd passed. Probably because fully sighted people didn't pay close attention to their other senses the way he did. He inhaled slowly, trying to figure out what the smell was. Or maybe it was a combination of smells. Whatever it was, it definitely didn't belong in the crisp desert air. The closest he could guess was that it was a machine, but not a clean one like the ones they had in the community. Its smell was strong and harsh. And there was also something sour and kind of familiar. Vomit?

He moved cautiously toward the smells, scanning the ground in front of and around him. His heartbeat quickened, but he stayed calm and focused, reminding himself he was still well within shouting distance of his friends.

Then he saw it: a machine, a vehicle with two wheels, leaned against a large rock.

And several feet from it was a body.

He stood still, listening. The voices of his friends faded in the distance, but he knew he could reach them easily if he took the road at a full run.

He moved closer to the body. It lay on its side, curled up. It wasn't large, but it wasn't a child. A woman. He didn't hear her breathing, but that didn't mean she wasn't. He squatted down beside her. The shadows from the bushes hid any useful information from his blurred outer vision, and he still didn't hear any breath coming from her.

Rafa had taught him that the heartbeat could be felt on the inside of the wrist. Teir pulled off a glove, and with his shaking hand, he explored the skin of the woman's upturned forearm for the spot he'd been shown, then carefully closed his hand around her wrist.

ten

Sadie sat across from the man at the small table. Surrounding them was a horde of people— yelling, arguing, waving fistfuls of money and betting slips in the air. On the center of the table between Sadie and the man was a revolver. A six-shooter. Inside the six-shooter was a solitary bullet. When it was your turn, the overseer spun the chamber like a roulette wheel—the origin of the game's moniker, Russian roulette. A game of chance. A game of hope. Unlike cards, there could be no skill honed in such a game. Spin the wheel and hope. Put the barrel to your head, pull the trigger, and hope you still saw the person across from you after the click. Hope the world didn't go black, and that the overseer would not be dragging your corpse aside before the frenzy of the crowd (a deafening roar of elation from those who won, a foot-stomping, obscenity-laced tirade from those that lost, and empathy from none) to be tossed into the pit filled with those before you who'd played and lost. Hope that you witnessed all of this happening to the one sitting across from you.

Unless you'd given up hope.

Unless each stack of money set before you was something that might have held significance a different lifetime ago, but was now only a reminder of how lucky you'd been thus far, that it was only a matter of time until it was your turn to be tossed into the pit by indifferent hands accompanied by indifferent shouts, taking with you the deceased mind that shared that same indifference and did not fear the bullet before it arrived—perhaps welcomed it in some way—the revelation as to why buried deeper and deeper with each spin of the chamber, each click of the trigger.

And so now, as Sadie stared at the man across the table from her, his face weathered and void of meaning, she wondered why he'd given up hope. Wondered, for that matter, why she too had given up hope. Pressed for an answer, she might admit it was a feeling more than anything she might hope to articulate. A hollowness. As if her insides had eroded over time, and she was now nothing but a wandering shell on a path that held no purpose. All roads led somewhere, didn't they? But if there was no purpose, perhaps they didn't.

It was Sadie's turn. The overseer spun the chamber. A hush fell over the crowd, the eagerness for results in their collective eyes akin to a pack of starving dogs hoping their owner might toss them a morsel.

Sadie raised the gun to her head, pressed the barrel to her temple. The crowd was one in anticipation. Her index finger massaged the trigger, stroking the lion before flicking it on the nose.

Please don't.

Huh? Sadie lowered the gun. The crowd murmured with confusion.

Let me show you something.

Sadie pushed back her chair and stood, gun now dangling at her side. She was not consciously using her gift, yet if the voice had been loud and true, wouldn't others have taken notice of the speaker? All eyes were on her; no heads were turning over shoulders wondering who dared speak such nonsense at such a pivotal time.

So it was in her head then, yes? Her conscience maybe?

No.

"Then what?" she blurted aloud.

Let me show you.

"Show me *what*?"

And though it did not happen, for Sadie it did: the crowd disappeared. The only one left standing was a boy, yet only just; the awkward throes of puberty had already begun to lengthen his bones and deepen his voice. He was cloaked in a garb that one might wear on a winter day, or so Sadie had read; winter was but a word in her world. When the boy pulled back his hood completely, long blond hair spilled out onto his ever-broadening shoulders; and his milky skin—truly the color of milk—was now on display. Yet the display was short-lived, for the aforementioned attributes became obsolete once the boy's eyes were revealed. The palest of blue, nearly translucent, they sat fixed in his pale, handsome face, never quite looking at you directly, yet somehow seeing you completely.

The boy held out his hand. Sadie left the table and went toward it. The crowd hollered their disapproval, yet they were still not visible to Sadie, just echoes that felt like a screaming wind trying to topple her.

She reached the boy. They were nearly equal in height—Sadie's five-seven to the boy's five-eight. Yes, it was apparent puberty had only just taken hold, but she still could not guess the boy's age; Cling had a way of expediting Mother Nature's plan.

Against her better judgment, Sadie took the boy's hand. She blinked, and they were gone, below ground, in a tunnel.

"How did you do that?" Sadie asked the boy.

The boy didn't respond. He turned and headed farther down the tunnel. Sadie followed.

"Hello?" she called to him. "How did you take me here? And where *is* here?"

The boy stopped and faced her, his pale blue eyes holding her face like hands.

Tell me if you see it, the boy said.

"See what?" Sadie asked.

The X I drew. Tell me if you see it.

Sadie frowned. "Can't *you* see it?"

Silence.

"I see it," she eventually said.

What do you see?

"I see a big blue X."

Strange. I drew my X in white.

"So what?"

Don't you want to know why it's now blue?

"Yeah—tell me."

Sadie blinked, and the boy was gone. She blinked again, and she was back at the table. It was her turn. She scanned the crowd for the boy, but he was nowhere. The overseer took the revolver and popped the chamber. He placed a solitary bullet inside. The bullet was blue. He spun the chamber, though Sadie knew it didn't matter where it landed—it was for her. She stood, and the overseer gripped her shoulder and shoved her back down.

"I don't want to play anymore," she said, eyes still scanning the room for the boy.

"Too late," the overseer said.

"Keep my money," Sadie said, starting to rise again. "I don't want to play anymore." Her eyes darted all over the crowded room: smoke, yelling, fistfuls of money in the air. No boy.

The overseer shoved her back down, more violently than before. "*Too late!*"

"Keep the money; I don't want to play anymore!"

The overseer popped the chamber again; all six holes were filled with blue bullets. "*TOO LATE!*"

Sadie leapt from the table, and the overseer grabbed her wrist.

eleven

The woman woke with a jolt, and Teir jumped back so fast he stumbled and fell, then scrambled away as quickly as he could. It reminded him of the first time he'd woken a sleeping dog.

Wait.

A dog?

The community had no dogs.

He'd heard stories about dogs, but he had no memory of ever meeting one. Yet the scene in his mind was so real. And he could see it clearly.

The woman spoke, startling him again. He pitched his gaze sideways to get a look at her. She sat not more than half a dozen feet from him, panting as if out of breath, her eyes wide and wild in the moonlight.

"Who are you?" she demanded.

"Who are *you*?" Teir shot back, trying hard not to sound as freaked out as he felt.

"Nobody," the woman said quickly.

"You always sleep on the side of the road, Nobody?"

The woman went to reply, but stopped and turned her head. "What are you looking at?" she asked.

Teir frowned. "Huh?"

"What's over there?"

"Where?"

"Where you're looking?"

He could hear that she was freaked out too. And irritated. He lowered his gaze to the ground and shook his head. "Nothing. I mean…what do *you* see?"

She hesitated. "I see only the desert night for miles." Her irritation gave way to suspicion. "And you?"

"Nothing."

"Then why the hell were you looking over there?"

"I was looking at *you*," he said.

"What, through your ears?"

Teir lifted his gaze and pitched it to the side again. "That's how I see, all right?"

"You can't look at me head on?"

Teir took a deep breath, pushed the hood from his head as he ran a shaking hand through his hair, and aimed his gaze toward her face. "There's something wrong with my vision. If I look at you, I can't see you, but if I look up or to the side, I can. Sort of. I'm not helpless, though. Not even close. So don't get any stupid ideas about trying to mess with me."

His words had come out angrier than he'd intended. He almost added more words to soften them but stopped himself. Though he didn't perceive any threat from her, she should know who she was dealing with. He turned his gaze so he could see her. Her eyes had gone wide again, and now her mouth hung open in obvious shock.

"It's *you*," she said. "I *know* you."

Teir frowned. She couldn't be serious. Was she teasing him? "What?"

"*I know you*," she repeated.

"I kinda doubt that."

She shook her head as if shaking off a punch. "No—I mean, I don't… I've *seen* you. In a dream. You took me somewhere, showed me things."

His heart began to pound, nearly drowning out the voice in his head calling him a fool.

She was crazy.

He was miles from home, all alone, and he'd just revealed his impairment to a lunatic.

He began to inch away from her. He'd been foolish to trust a stranger, and though confident in his ability to defend himself if push came to shove, he was wise enough to know when to run like hell. He gathered his feet beneath him and rose to a crouch, preparing to crash through the bushes and take off down the road toward his friends.

Then the woman spoke again.

"You took me to a tunnel. There was a big blue *X* on the wall. An *X you* claimed to have drawn yourself." She paused, as if struggling to remember. "Except you said you hadn't drawn the *X* in blue, you'd drawn it in white."

Teir flashed on past grammar lessons with Rafa, words used when asking questions to gather information. The five *W*s: who, what, when, where, and why. They swirled in his head without order, and he struggled with which to select to begin gathering that information.

He ended up gathering none. A far more urgent word shot its way up to the front of the line, cutting in front of the five *W*s.

How?

How could this woman possibly have known about the tunnel? But more than that, how could she have known about the *X* he'd drawn? No one knew about that. Not even Rafa.

The five *W*s began to trickle into place: He'd drawn the *X* in white chalk. So *why* did the woman say it was blue? And if she'd been in the tunnel as she claimed, *when* was that? He'd drawn the *X* only yesterday. *Who* was this woman? And *what* the heck was she—

Teir's train of thought took a sudden detour. *How* had jumped to the front of the line again. And this was immediately followed by a dawning revelation that saw only one of the five *W*s fit to join *how*.

Who?

Who was this woman, and *how* did she know what couldn't be known?

The answer to both questions was the same. She was a martyr.

twelve

"*A martyr...*" the boy said with breathless excitement, as though he'd just found all the world's remaining pockets of Clear. "You're a martyr."

Sadie immediately got to her feet and began dusting herself off. The kid was one hell of a mystery, yes, and she desperately wanted answers from him, but he'd uttered the M-word. For all she knew, this kid had been sent by the Blue's warlord after word got out about what she'd done back at the tavern. What was it she'd dreamt? A blue *X*? A blue *X this* kid had drawn? Her gift often leaked into her dreams, but always with frustrating ambiguity, giving her more riddle than fact. In her dream, the kid seemed to want to help her. And he *did* look truly startled and amazed when Sadie gave an account of her fever dream. Would a warlord—more gluttony than guile, all of them—really create such an elaborate ruse, such a convincing pawn like this boy, just to find a martyr? To exact revenge if the boy was, in fact, a fledgling henchman for the Blue?

Sadie continued dusting herself off, her blasé manner a play at indifference to the boy's words. "No idea what you're talking about."

The kid was sharp; he saw through her act and pressed harder. He stood, eyes facing east again as though addressing a ghost. "A martyr," he said. "Someone who can *see*."

"I guess that rules you out."

Previous mention of the boy's disability had sparked an immediate response. This time the boy went on as though he hadn't heard Sadie, his excitement immunizing him to her goading. "My friend taught me all about people like you," he said. "You're called martyrs because you endure suffering whenever you use your gift of sight. 'Witness'—that's what 'martyr' means in Late Greek. Did you know that? 'Witness.'"

"Well, aren't you just a sponge for knowledge."

The boy continued, more eager than ever, the words not coming out fast enough. "My friend told me that the true definition—the today one, the uh…the one we use today—it means one who suffers great pain in order to further a belief or principle."

Sadie shrugged. "Well, that's where you're wrong then, kiddo. My principles are as sturdy as a drunk, and any beliefs I might have had kicked me in the guts long ago."

"I was just giving you what was written in the book," the boy said. "Rafa explained to me why the definition in the book came to stick to people like you."

"Rafa?"

"My friend."

Sadie nodded. She wanted to leave. To hop on her motorhorse and be far from here. How a Blue, or any other unsavory character, had not happened upon her when she was unconscious on the side of the road was nothing shy of a miracle.

But her dream. Her damned dream and the riddle it produced. A riddle with one heck of a major clue that just happened to be standing before her, certain she was a martyr. And he was likely a mole, no less. The pale skin, the shrouded attire, the long hair that Sadie guessed needn't be a common trait among male moles—yet logic told her such a look would never be braved by anyone above ground save for a bitch whose keeper happened to fancy long hair on his man.

And of course the eyes. The palest of blue. Were they a product of his environment, or had nature granted them to the boy? And then there was the affliction those eyes came with: his unusual way of seeing—or not seeing. The irony of the one person finding her on the side of the road being a boy with poor sight was not lost on Sadie. In time she might laugh about it.

Time.

Every man or woman's time above ground was subject to Cling, or the lawlessness that could take you that much sooner. The moment Sadie's bullets had hit the member of the Blue back at that tavern, she'd all but turned an hourglass over, the grains of sand blue.

Just like the bullets in the chamber of the six-shooter, yes?

Yes. No riddle there; the metaphor in that part of the dream was clear.

Just like the blue X *on the tunnel wall? The boy who took you there to see it?*

Big riddle there.

"Tell me where that tunnel is," Sadie said to the boy.

"What?"

"The tunnel with the blue *X*. Tell me where it is."

"It's *not* a blue *X*. It's white. I drew it in white."

"Just tell me."

"I can take you there."

"I'd rather you just tell me."

"You'd never find it on your own."

"If you give me the whereabouts, I can do the rest."

"By using your gift? Your martyr gift?"

Sadie said nothing.

"I won't tell you, but I *will* show you," he said. "And if I do, you have to promise to help us."

"Who's 'us'?"

"My community. We need the help of a martyr."

"You a mole?"

"Huh?"

"If you're a mole, I'll forgive your ignorance, no wind below ground and all. But if you're not, you should know that up here the wind has ears. That word you keep babbling on about can attract all sorts of people you'd rather not be attractive to."

The boy paused and dropped his head in thought, as if accessing some hidden file. He then lifted his head, a confused look on his face. "A mole is a small mammal that lives below ground and eats insects."

Sadie gave a small splay of her hands as if waiting for her opponent to acknowledge checkmate. "Sounds like you just gave me an autobiography, kiddo."

"Teir."

"Huh?"

"My name's Teir."

"As in what comes out of your eyes when you cry?"

He frowned. "T-E-I-R. Short for Teiresias. It's an ancient name. From Greek mythology."

"It'd be easier if I could just call you kiddo."

"If you want me to answer, you should call me Teir."

Sadie nodded slowly, something that felt like a smirk itching at the corner of her mouth for the kid's quick wit. She was starting to warm to the idea that he *was* indeed a mole, and no warlord pawn. No threat. Still, certainty was for dead men.

(*So do it. Get in his head.*)

I just spent the last however many hours passed out on the side of the road for the taking. You think I want that to happen again?

(*Cut it off before you get too sick.*)

I'd have to touch him. Can't get inside anyone's head without touching them. It's not like reading cards or finding Clear.

(*So touch him.*)

He doesn't look like the type who likes to be touched.

(*So then knock him the hell out and do it while he's snoozing.*)

I don't know...

(*Okay, then what?—you gonna trust this kid to guide you wherever he wants? Could be right into a warlord's arms, for all you know. The* Blue *warlord's arms.*)

I don't know. I think he's a mole.

(*Since when do you think this long? Your gut has always served you better than your*

brain.)

Wasn't thinking back at that tavern; now I've got a bull's-eye on my back. Scratch that; I'm a bottle of whiskey with a bull's-eye label. They'll suck me dry before gunning me down.

Sadie threw a leg over her motorhorse and flicked her chin over her shoulder. "Get on," she told him.

The kid's excitement was everywhere. He instantly looked up toward the night sky—obviously his preferred angle of peripheral vision when mobile—and hurried as fast as he could towards the vehicle. He hopped on behind Sadie, bouncing the suspension. "Will you go fast?" he asked.

"Just tell me where to go."

"North. We need to catch up with my friends first. I need to tell them to turn around and head back."

"What?"

"A small group from my community is heading north. That's who I was following when I found you." He then paused for a tick, as though owning up to a lie. "I kinda wasn't supposed to be following them."

"Tunnel first," Sadie said. "You can get your friends later."

Sadie felt the boy stiffen behind her.

"Friends first," he said. "Friends first or no tunnel."

Such loyalty. A trait as elusive above ground as happiness. Either the kid *was* a mole, and the rumors about their virtuous way of life below ground were true, or the boy was attempting to lead her into the lion's den.

By telling you about it first? Not the wisest of ways to set a trap.

(*Just get inside the damn kid's head already.*)

I just need to have him get me close. I'll dump him and do the rest myself.

(*The kid's not gonna let you go an inch without finding his people first.*)

Sadie sighed. "Fine," she said. "We'll go north first. Hold on to my waist."

Teir wrapped both arms around her waist. She reached down and took hold of one of his hands, entering his mind…

thirteen

Like the fever dreams that riddle Sadie with only snippets of second sight, so too is the result of entering one's mind. Too many memories; too many doors. If she is lucky, the recent memories will not yet have a door. They will swirl overhead and around her like loose pages in a book, waiting to be assembled and bound behind a door of their own.

And for this boy Teir they do. And Sadie is grateful. Bound memories are deep, and for each door she opens, so too will her sickness grow deep. She need only know whether the boy is trustworthy. Tonight, a few pages of recent memory flutter down and before her eyes where they will reveal not single images, but scenes.

She absorbs them into her own mind, and soon all doors fade away, all other pages floating and swirling above dissolve, and soon there is only the recent pages she has selected, coming to life around her as she observes, unnoticed, another person's life. Several facts present themselves over the course of Sadie's stay:

The boy is indeed a mole.

The boy is indeed a member of a loving community. An *advanced* community, all things considered. Certainly more advanced than the world above.

The boy is loved and cared for.

The boy is…a mystery to his own people.

What?

The memory is gone. Sadie snatches another swirling page from above, enters another time in the boy's life. More facts:

The boy was not born in this community below ground. He was...

What?

Found.

Found? Found where?

Sadie snatches more pages. They reveal nothing but more recent memories: friendly gatherings; meals; lessons with his friend Rafa; exploring tunnels.

Tunnels!

Could she find the tunnel with the blue *X* now? Yes.

More pages of memory. The tunnel is there. The boy is there, drawing his white—not blue, *not* blue—*X*. Sadie cannot unearth the whereabouts of the tunnel from her current location because the boy himself does not know; she is limited by his conscious knowledge. It looks as if she *will* need him after all. He is a mole. He is no threat. He is—

A mystery to his own people.

Sadie has the information she needs. But the doors further down the corridor of the boy's mind beckon.

He was found. What does that mean?

Sadie cautiously strolls down the corridor of the boy's mind, each memory another step back in time. She can feel the sickness growing inside her as she goes.

Many doors reveal fond memories much like the loose pages had; however, there is one constant throughout. A constant she had noticed in the loose pages at the start of the corridor yet had initially dismissed. Now she is forced to address this constant as she discovers it is not something recent, but stretches back years, starting shortly after the boy's arrival in the community: Nightmares plague the boy, their content always gone the moment he wakes.

She opens another door. The answer to *found* is there: discovered as a child under a creosote bush, unconscious and near death. He is wearing an iron collar and shackles. The visual to this memory is murky as the boy does not remember it well; it is his own re-creation of events as dictated to him over the years by his friend Rafa.

Is this the answer to the nightmares? Yes and no. Being shackled and left for dead, horrific as it is, is only the culmination of the boy's ordeal.

What preceded it? She had to know.

Don't.

She'd never attempted to dig for a dream before, had not, in fact, spent this much time inside someone's head before.

Don't.

Sadie's fever is exceptionally strong now, but still she moves on. The corridor's end is in sight. But how is that possible? There is still so much to know. How is the end in sight already?

And then the answer—shamefully obvious, once realized—presents itself to her:

Because the boy himself doesn't know.

Sadie arrives at the final door. It is not on either side of her as all of the other doors had been during her trek; it is directly in front of her, the corridor narrowing to a point that is the final door, the door that the boy himself had never opened, for he did not have the capability to open it. A door of suppressed memories is often forever locked to the owner. The deeper the trauma, the trickier the lock.

Except this is not Sadie's door. She is a visitor. The handle will turn for her.

DON'T.

Sadie opens the door and enters. Her extreme sickness that follows pales in comparison to her experience inside.

fourteen

Rafa heard a rhythmic sound behind them steadily growing louder. Running feet. He turned quickly to behold a sight that sent a chill through him.

Izar spoke. "For the love of all creation, that's—"

Teir stumbled as he reached them and Rafa caught him, the boy's forward momentum nearly knocking them both to the ground. Rafa held tight, trying to steady him, but it seemed as if Teir's sense of balance had completely abandoned him. His whole body shook with tremors more violent than any Rafa had ever observed before. His breath came in short bursts that sounded painful. Rafa feared he was having a seizure.

Rafa dragged Teir to a large rock, and they sat together. Teir began to mumble incoherently between gasps for breath.

"Calm down," Rafa said into the clump of hair over his friend's ear.

"Please help her," Teir eventually managed.

"Who?" Rafa asked.

Teir's only response was to press his face into Rafa's shoulder and let loose a few quiet sobs as his body continued to shake.

"Tell me what's going on," Rafa pleaded.

It was several moments before the boy caught his breath and regained some semblance of composure.

"Who needs our help, Teir?" Izar asked.

He lifted his gaze and stared down the road in the direction from which he'd come. His expression was one Rafa had never seen him wear in all the years they'd known each other.

Unmitigated terror.

Rafa did not dare imagine what could possibly frighten him to such a degree. Teir feared nothing.

"Who needs our help?" Rafa pressed gently.

Teir shook his head, brow wrinkling in thought as if he was trying to remember. Rafa fought to suppress his growing concern that something was going very wrong in his friend's troubled young mind; that Rafa's departure on this expedition coupled with the boy's traumatic past had triggered some sort of psychotic break.

Moments passed as the small group of travelers stood awaiting his response.

Then, softly: "*My mother.*"

"Where is she?" Rafa asked, dreading the answer beyond all measure.

Teir blinked rapidly as fresh tears rolled down his cheeks, glistening like stardust in the bright moonlight. "She's dead."

Rafa had never been so grateful for his sister's compassion and directness as he was in the moments that followed, for he had no words of his own.

Izar lowered herself to one knee in front of Teir and took the boy's hand in hers. "I'm so sorry, little brother," she said carefully, as if speaking to a much younger child. "This world is a cruel place, and we've all lost people we love. But sweetheart, what on earth are you doing out here?"

Again the group stood quietly awaiting his response. Rafa watched Teir lift his sightless gaze to the night sky as a revelation seemed to illuminate the boy's pale, tear-streaked face.

His voice was a whisper nearly carried away on the desert wind.

"I found a martyr."

. . .

The group made their way quickly back down the road with Teir in the lead. Rafa watched him march: long strides, head down, hands shoved deep into the pockets of his hoodie, speaking only when spoken to, answers coming in a low, sharp monotone.

"How do you know she's a martyr?" Izar asked for the third time in ten minutes, clearly unsatisfied with Teir's terse non-answers, which had nonetheless convinced the group to follow him.

"She knows things," Teir said, apparently worn down by Izar's persistence. "And stop saying that word—the M-word. She said it's dangerous to say it."

"Fine. What things does she know?" Izar asked.

"Things she shouldn't know."

"Such as?"

Teir hesitated, picking up his pace as if he could silence Izar by lengthening the distance between them.

Izar, of course, would not be ignored. "Answer me, Teiresias."

Another moment of defiant silence preceded his response. "Things about me."

"About your past?"

Teir halted abruptly and spun around to face her wearing a look of grim fury, another expression Rafa had never seen on him. It altered the boy's appearance in an alarming way, aging him by what seemed like decades. Rafa hoped it was not a glimpse of the man Teir would someday become.

"*No*," Teir shot back. "About my life now. Things I've never told anyone, ever."

Rafa felt wounded by this disclosure. The clinician in him knew that an important stage of adolescence was the formation of an identity that was separate from that of a child's parents. For all intents and purposes, and despite there being only six years between them, Rafa was Teir's adoptive parent. But were they not also brothers? Best friends? What secrets could Teir possibly feel the need to keep from Rafa?

Before Rafa could ponder further, Teir turned back around and continued his forward march. "It's not much farther. Look for the tracks of the machine she was riding on the right. They lead into a break in the bushes."

.   .   .

Rafa knelt down beside the unconscious woman and placed a hand to her forehead. She was burning with fever. He quickly removed his pack, dampened a cloth with water from his canteen, and began to gently press it to her face.

"What's her name, Teir?" Izar asked.

"I don't know."

"Where is she from?"

"I don't know."

"What *do* you know about her?"

Teir hesitated before his next evasive response. "She said she'll help us if we take her to the community."

Rafa spoke without looking up. "We must either find shelter before daybreak or carry her back to the community. I'd rather treat her at the clinic. Her fever is very high, and there's little I can do for her out here."

"Then we'll carry her," Izar said. "We've got five strong men among us to take turns handing her off."

Teir quickly stepped back. "I'm not touching her!"

Rafa looked up, startled and shocked by Teir's sudden outburst. He stood and handed the damp cloth to Izar. "Keep her face wet." Then he stepped over to Teir, gently took him by the arm, and led him far enough from the group for a private conversation.

Teir spoke first, keeping his gaze on the ground in front of him. "Please don't make me touch her, Rafa."

"You know that I would never force you to do something you did not want to do. And you know that if anyone ever tried to force you to do something, Izar and I would defend your right to refuse, as you would do for both of us." Teir nodded, and Rafa continued: "If this woman is indeed a…the type of individual we're seeking, and if she is indeed willing to help us, then we should accept her assistance. However—" Rafa paused for a moment to deflect an unexpected flare of emotion. "If she has hurt you in *any* way…"

"She didn't hurt me. She's grouchy and paranoid and spooky, but I think that's just because of…you know…what she is. It's just…" He paused, struggling with his words. "When I first found her, I couldn't tell if she was alive, so I touched her wrist to check, like you showed me, and I had this…memory."

"Of what?"

"A dog."

"A *dog*?"

"Yeah. A huge white dog with a giant mouth and blue eyes. I remembered accidentally waking it up from a sound sleep, and it was startled, and it scared me half to death." He paused. "I could *see* it, Rafa. *Clearly*."

Rafa had always suspected that there had been a time in Teir's childhood before his vision had deteriorated, during which he could see with perfect clarity. Hereditary forms of central vision loss, even the rare types which affected young children, were almost always progressive, their onset preceded by a period in which the individual's vision was normal. Rafa had never shared this information with Teir, though. Why go into clinical detail when it would only serve to underscore all the boy had lost?

Teir continued, his voice quiet, as if merely speaking the words unnerved him. "Then when I got on her machine with her, to ride and catch up with you and tell you to turn around, I...had a nightmare. Except I wasn't asleep." Again he paused before forcing his words out at barely a whisper. "And I remembered some of it."

For as long as Teir had been plagued by his dreams, Rafa had wanted to know as much about them as possible, as if having enough data would lead him to a cure for the affliction. It was a problem he wanted to solve almost as much as he wanted to find a cure for Cling. But his mind flashed on Teir's terror-stricken face glistening in the moonlight not an hour ago, and the last thing Rafa wanted to do was poke at that raw wound in his friend's psyche while they were so far from the comfort and privacy of home.

Izar's voice cut through his conflicted rumination. "Let's get a move on. We've got a lot of ground to cover with some heavy cargo, and daybreak isn't far off."

. . .

There was little conversation during the journey home. Izar led the way, holding her large rifle in front of her instead of slung across her back. Teir silently pushed the martyr's two-wheeled machine as the other men took turns carrying her. While Rafa held her in his arms, try as he might to detect them, he experienced no peculiar sensations or visions at all. Her persistently raging fever was all he felt, evoking concern in him for the well-being of his patient, but nothing more. Determined to subdue his churning thoughts, he occupied his mind by meticulously detailing the methods and remedies he would use to care for her back at the clinic.

They arrived with moments to spare before daybreak. The woman was still unconscious, and Rafa set to work quickly, using fans and cool compresses to manage her fever, and then preparing a variety of tinctures to administer once she regained consciousness. Izar reported on their journey to the community's elders, including a vague but acceptable description of how Teir found the woman and why he believed her to be a martyr, which pacified Julen and Elixa enough to spare the boy their displeasure at his recklessness for running off into the desert night alone.

All the while, Teir sat silently at the woman's bedside, appearing to stare at her motionless body as though he could clearly see every detail. The dark smudges beneath his pale eyes had deepened, but his face gave nothing away. He looked as though he'd turned to stone.

"Why don't you go home and get some sleep," Rafa suggested gently.

The shake of Teir's head in refusal was almost imperceptible.

"Are you hungry?"

Another slight shake of the head.

Rafa hesitated before his next question, unsure of how to phrase it or even whether the time was right to ask. "Would you like to talk about what you remembered from your dream?"

Though his unseeing gaze remained locked on the martyr and his expression remained blank, Teir's lips parted, and he inhaled slowly, and Rafa thought he might speak.

Then the woman opened her eyes.

fifteen

Finn and Vidar in Vidar's chamber. Moans of agony in the distance as the two men sat sipping whiskey by candlelight.

Vidar sipped from his cup and leaned back with a sigh in the giant high-back chair, one custom-made to accommodate his frame. "I usually take no pleasure in the torment of others," he said. Then, with a sly smirk: "I took pleasure in that."

"Your hand has tasted blood on plenty of occasions," Finn said.

"Business, my friend. Always business."

The moans grew from the deepest parts of the chamber.

"So you're done with them then?" Finn asked, finishing the last of his whiskey in a gulp.

Vidar leaned forward and poured his friend more. "Oh no," he replied. "Not remotely." He topped off his own cup and leaned back in his chair once again. "A few of my men have located an exceptionally thriving mound far out into the wastelands. At least five feet in diameter and as high as my knee."

"Mound?"

"Fire ants," Vidar said. "It will be interesting to see if the inhabitants of that mound, once properly disturbed, can envelop those poor fools completely."

Finn's eyes widened. He then raised his cup and said: "I am *very* glad we are on the same side."

Vidar released his trademark laugh. Its echo in his chambers seemed to catch the array of candles throughout, causing their flames to bend and dance before burning tall once again.

They sat quiet for a moment, sipping their whiskey, moans in the distance as wavering as the candlelight.

"I've been thinking," Finn eventually said.

"Dangerous," Vidar said with a smile.

Finn returned a quick courtesy smile, eager to continue. "This martyr...I have an idea who it might be."

"Oh?"

"All accounts say it was a woman who's good with a pistol. How many martyrs you ever hear about that were fighters?"

Vidar's response was an agreeable nod. "So who is she?"

"If I'm right, her name is Sadie. Wily as they come."

"And you know her how?"

"Past interests."

"In each other?" Vidar asked with a little smile.

Finn bypassed the implication, even though there was some truth to it. "Locating bounties."

"Using a martyr to find your man? That's cheating, Finley," Vidar joked.

"It was Sadie herself who once told me cheaters always win."

Vidar's laughter erupted in the chamber again. When it passed, he finished his whiskey and set the cup aside. "Get to your point, Finn. The mound is waiting."

"The three of us would like nothing more than to see the Blue wiped out for good. You and I for obvious reasons; Sadie, out of self-preservation."

"You propose we find her and utilize her gift to help infiltrate the Blue's compound at its weak points, is that it?" Vidar asked.

"Yes. No martyr would ever be willing to use their gift to help us. Hell, no martyr would ever give up their *identity* to us. But here we have someone we *know* to be a martyr, and someone who has all the incentive in the world to see the Blue destroyed. An opportunity like this is as rare as an endless vein of Clear."

Vidar stood. Turned and stared quietly at his shrine for a spell. His massive fist was soon clenched at his side. Finn had seen battle maces less intimidating.

He turned back to Finn. "Find out if the martyr truly is this Sadie you know. If it is, bring her back here, and the three of us will talk."

Finn frowned. "Finding out if the martyr is Sadie won't be too bad. But actually finding *her*? She's a martyr in hiding. One step below a ghost."

Vidar took a step forward, placed a hand on Finn's shoulder. All traces of his jovial manner were now gone as was often the case when reliving the past. Finn did not take it personally, but it was no less unsettling.

"Then I suppose you won't be able to cheat on this one, my friend," Vidar said. "Although I do expect you to win all the same."

Finn nodded. "I always do."

sixteen

Sadie opened her eyes. Even though her vision swam and the surrounding light seemed akin to that of a cave's, she was certain she did not know the face hovering above, tending to her. Certain, because only one person had ever tended to Sadie in her lifetime, and she was not looking in a mirror.

She offered a feeble chuckle up at her caregiver. "Like poking holes in a bucket, genius." She chuckled again, triggering a cough she was too weak to cover with her hand.

"I'm sorry?" her caregiver asked.

It was a man's voice. A *polite* man's voice. It didn't fit. Sadie carried on anyway.

"Getting me well just to make me sick again," she said. "Why even bother?"

"Why would we get you sick again?" the man asked. He sounded genuinely interested, concerned. The antithesis of the snarky condescension she would have expected from a member of the Blue.

"It's Clear you're after, yes?" Sadie asked.

"Teir explained it to you?"

Teir… why did she know the name?

Sadie closed her eyes again. "What's to explain? You want revenge for your fellow mouth-breather, and you want Clear. Pretty easy math."

"Do you know math?" the caregiver asked, again sounding genuinely interested.

"Yeah, I do. Me dead, plus you Clear, equals happy Blue assholes."

"There she goes with the color blue again," a second male voice said.

Sadie opened her eyes. Her direct line of sight was no less clear, yet her peripheral vision was informative, and none too surprisingly. It was a trick she'd learned while roaming the desert at night. The dark played tricks on direct line of sight; only peripheral vision had ever proved true in catching enough to let her live another day. And so now her peripheral vision rewarded her with the hazy silhouette of a second male keeping what appeared to be a cautious vigil by the foot of her bed.

The second male would not look at her directly, only kept his profile to her, as if he too knew the benefits of peripheral vision in the dark.

"That's how I see, all right?"

These words…coming back to Sadie like the blinding flash of a migraine. She closed her eyes tight, grimacing in pain. The caregiver wiped her brow with the damp cloth.

You can't look at me head on? Her own voice now, though just as brutal in thrumming the pulse behind her eyes.

"There's something wrong with my vision." His words again. *"If I look at you, I can't see you, but if I look up or to the side, I can. Sort of. I'm not helpless, though. Not even close. So don't get any stupid ideas about trying to mess with me…"*

Sadie risked opening her eyes. The caregiver was immediate with the damp cloth again. The second male at the foot of her bed had not moved, kept his profile to her—

"That's how I see, all right?"

—that profile now giving Sadie the tracing of long hair in his silhouette, and suddenly she recalled thinking that long hair would never be braved by anyone above ground save for a bitch whose keeper happened to fancy such a look on his man—

"I'm not helpless, though. Not even close. So don't get any stupid ideas about trying to mess with me…"

—and this kid seemed anything but a bitch.

This kid…kiddo…it'd be easier if I could just call you kiddo.

"If you want me to answer, you should call me Teir."

Sadie closed her eyes once again and smirked. "Teir," she said. "Short for Teiresias. An ancient name from Greek mythology." She opened her eyes and looked up at the caregiver. To say the caregiver looked rattled was like saying Cling was a scourge.

"Yes...yes, that's right," the caregiver said, glancing over at Teir.

Teir did not seem to share the caregiver's surprise. His stone expression remained, his spot still rooted by the foot of the bed, out of arm's reach.

"Are you Rafa?" Sadie asked the caregiver.

"I am, yes. I'm glad you've regained your senses. You had us worried there for a spell."

Sadie grunted as she tried propping herself up on her elbows. "Sense is something I've been woefully lacking in as of late, Mr. Rafa."

"Rafa is my nickname," he said. "It's short for Rafael. My full name is Rafael Carrera Allende."

"You people really got the names, don't you?"

Rafa smiled. "And your name is?"

"Sadie."

"Do you have a surname?"

"You mean like yours? Hereditary names passed down through generations?"

Rafa nodded.

"No."

Her curtness tugged at his smile some. Still the respectful host, Rafa said: "Okay...well, it's a pleasure to meet you, Sadie. There are many others here who would like to meet you as well—"

Sadie held up a hand, cutting Rafa off. "I'd like some alone time with the boy before I do anything."

Rafa glanced over at Teir.

Teir nodded back at his friend. "I'll be okay."

Rafa left them alone.

seventeen

Sadie grunted some more as she attempted to prop herself further up on her elbows. "I feel weak as a damn kitten," she said. "You ever seen a kitten before?"

Teir said nothing.

"No, of course not," she said. Then, casting Teir a knowing glance: "Seen a dog though, right? Big white one with a million teeth?" She smirked and added: "One that doesn't take kindly to being disturbed while it's sleeping?"

Teir approached, his stone expression now tight lips and a frown. "How did you…what did you *do* to me?"

Sadie gave up trying to support herself on her elbows and slid back down the bed with a flop of the head and a sigh. "I wish I knew, kiddo."

"I told you not to call me that."

Sadie chuckled and held out an apologetic hand. Teir hopped back as though her hand was a flame. "Don't touch me!"

Sadie withdrew her hand and folded it across her chest with the other. "I can understand you being so upset; I would be too if I'd just recalled a memory buried so deep…buried so deep for good reason."

Teir's frown diffused, his tight lips now moving without coherent words, as if his mind and voice were out of sync—and they were.

"Don't bother looking for the right questions, because I don't have the answers," Sadie said. "As soon as I think I've got this curse figured out, it whacks me over the head with something new." She closed her eyes and sighed again, keeping them closed as she spoke. "I've poked around in heads before—nothing new there—but I lingered in yours the longest, dug the deepest. You have some seriously repressed shit in there, and I guess you could say my curiosity got the better of my common sense." She opened her eyes and lifted her head, locking her gaze on Teir's profile. Her expression was somber, her tone as apologetic as Sadie ever got. "If I would've known that my digging would have allowed you to see too, I would have never done it. Sorry, kiddo."

Teir did not object to her use of "kiddo" this time. He didn't even seem to notice it. His pale blue eyes were fixed elsewhere, and Sadie knew it was not his unique way of seeing that fixed them off of her and onto something else; he was not seeing anything in the room at all.

Teir's gaze snapped, and he shook his head angrily. "I can't see it clearly! I was little, and my vision was bad, but I saw these men…I saw these men, and they were torturing my mother, and she…died. They tortured her to death."

"What else do you see?"

"I don't know. I see more, but it's hazy. I—" He stopped suddenly. "What did *you* see? You saw it too, right? What did *you* see?"

"I'm only capable of seeing what you saw," Sadie lied. "If you're hazy, I'm hazy."

"Fine, then tell me what you saw; I'll tell you if I saw the same."

Sadie shook her head. "Trust me, kiddo, we saw the same."

Again Teir ignored "kiddo" for more pressing matters. "You knew about the white dog with the big mouth and blue eyes…"

"So?"

"Why do you remember *that* so clearly?"

Why did she mention the damn dog? She certainly wasn't trying to stir anything in the boy; his curiosity churned just fine on its own.

Another hiccup of self-destruction perhaps? Flaunting your gift, consequences be damned?

"Because *you* remember it clearly," she said. "The memory was less traumatic, easier to release."

Teir began to pace around the room. He stopped abruptly and lunged for Sadie's bedside with an outstretched hand. "Do it again!"

Now it was Sadie who recoiled as though a flame were thrust at her. "Are you nuts?!"

Teir thrust his arm forward again, adamant. "I don't care—just do it."

Sadie scooched away from him. "I'm not doing it, kiddo—sorry."

Teir let his arm drop. "Then why did you tell Rafa you wanted to be alone with me?"

"To apologize."

"You're lying," Teir said.

"The tunnel," Sadie said. "You promised to take me to the tunnel with the blue *X*."

"*White X*. And only if you helped my people."

"I said I would."

"*I'm* one of my people. Help me."

Sadie smirked at the boy's quick reasoning. "I agreed to help you find Clear. That's all."

Teir remained rooted at her bedside, refusing to budge.

"Why not just give it a little time?" Sadie said. "Perhaps more will come to you."

Teir spun and left without another word.

Rafa entered shortly after and approached Sadie's bedside. His concerned expression held blatant tells of protective accusation. "Teir just stormed past me in the hall," he said. "What did you do to him?"

"It's what I *didn't* do to him," Sadie said.

Rafa's concerned frown became a quizzical one. "Come again?"

"He wanted me to get in his head again," Sadie said. "I said no. He got angry and left."

A moment of pause. Rafa's initial confrontational manner for Teir's safety had now dissolved. "What *did* you do to him?" he asked again, his voice soft and unchallenging this time.

Sadie sighed. "In my infinite stupidity, I unlocked a memory in the kid that would bring even the hardiest bounty hunter to his knees."

"His mother's death," Rafa said quietly.

"Right, only he doesn't remember it all just yet."

"How do you know?"

"He told me—said it was still hazy. The only thing he seems sure about is that his mother was tortured to death."

"Did *you* see it?" Rafa asked. "His memories?"

"I told him I saw what he saw. If he saw hazy, then I saw hazy."

Rafa cocked his head. "Is that true?"

Sadie paused, considering her next words. Her gut told her Rafa was trustworthy, but her apprehension for telling him the truth was truth itself. It formed bonds. Sadie likened bonds to Cling—it weakened you over time, made you ignore your gut in favor of the heart. Still, she saw no harm in telling Rafa what she'd actually seen; she'd come this far. "Sort of," she said, followed by a long sigh. "It *was* hazy, but if all he saw was his mother being tortured to death, then I definitely saw more than he did. I don't know how, but I did."

Rafa looked away for a tick, ruminating. When he came to, he said: "Did you see how he escaped?"

"What does it matter?"

"Because it's nothing short of miraculous. How does a five or six-year-old boy, beaten, shackled, and near-starved, escape brutal captors on his own and traverse the wastelands?"

"He had help," Sadie said. "A young man, maybe a slave, I don't know."

"What happened to the young man?"

"Got bit by a snake and died."

"Leaving Teir alone in the desert."

"Yup."

Rafa looked away again. Turned back and said: "We should tell him."

Sadie snorted. "It's been my experience that some memories are better left buried."

"These memories," Rafa began, "they *haunt* him. He has constant nightmares, yet he never remembers them. It torments him. Revealing to Teir what actually happened during his childhood would be a vital step forward in his healing."

Sadie shrugged. "Do whatever you want; it's got nothing to do with me."

Rafa recoiled. "How can you say that? It has *everything* to do with you."

"I didn't ask the kid to touch me."

"Oh, I see—better he should have left you on the side of the road to die?"

"All I'm saying is that from the moment that kid touched me, it triggered some chain of events that I don't—and don't *want* to—understand. He said he can help me find a tunnel in exchange for some Clear for you guys. I'm willing to do that."

"Tunnel?" Rafa said. "What tunnel?"

"No idea. But I dreamt about it. The kid was there. He'd drawn a blue *X* on it, and this was only moments after I was about to blow my own head off with a gun full of blue bullets."

Rafa gave a quizzical frown, started to ask for elaboration—

"Don't ask," Sadie said, beating him to the punch. "Point is, the kid said the tunnel is real, and I have a pretty good idea of what my dream was trying to tell me."

"And that is?"

"Doesn't matter. Me and the kid had a deal. He gets me to the tunnel, I find you guys some Clear."

Rafa gave the quizzical frown again, clearly digesting something that wasn't going down right. "This dream you had about Teir, about the tunnel, is that what released his memories?"

"No, that was an accident. He hopped on the back of my motorhorse, touched me again, and boom—good times."

"And yet I carried you all the way here and experienced no such phenomena," Rafa said.

"Consider yourself lucky."

A moment of pause as the two of them considered one another, the vastly different means by which their intelligence was honed coming to a point here and now.

"Tell me," Rafa eventually said, "why did you agree to help Teir?"

"I already told you; he said he'd show me the tunnel in exchange for Clear."

"Using your gift makes you ill, does it not?"

"It does."

"Yet you're willing to get ill again just to help us?"

Sadie shook her head, annoyed. "I thought moles understood English. *I am getting you some damn Clear in exchange for the damn boy showing me the damn tunnel.* You think I'd get sick for nothing in return?"

"Could you not just use your gift to find this tunnel *without* Teir's help?"

"Maybe. It would take longer, though. Besides, why get sick if the kid is willing to show me?"

"But you'll just end up getting sick anyway—when you help us locate some Clear."

Sadie frowned. "What the hell are you getting at?"

"If you chose to use your gift to find this tunnel on your own, you would get sick, yes?"

"Yeah."

"If you chose to let Teir show you instead in exchange for some Clear, you would *still* get sick when it came time to locating that Clear, yes?"

"Yeah…"

"Either way, you would get sick, except you chose the option of helping us rather than going it alone. You have honor, Sadie."

Sadie snorted. "You don't know how this 'gift' works. Know why? Because even *I* don't. But after thirty-five years, what I *do* know is that it's not as easy as closing your eyes and receiving some detailed map bigger than life. The closer you are to something, the stronger the premonition. Even when looking for Clear for my own personal use, I need to wander on my motorhorse, sometimes for days before I get a sense of something." She broke eye contact, looked at the ceiling. "Hell, I was even planning on dumping the boy once he got me close enough to the tunnel. That sound honorable to you?"

"Why didn't you?"

"Because I got into his head and lingered too long. Got sick again. I was stupid."

"I don't believe you would have dumped Teir. I believe you would have kept going, made good on the deal the two of you agreed upon."

She snorted again. "This tunnel I keep mentioning? The one the boy knows about?"

"Yes?"

"My gut tells me it leads directly beneath the compound of a gang known as the Blue. The reason that information is important to me is because I would very much like to follow that tunnel, sneak into the Blue compound, and murder their warlord in cold blood." Sadie then pointed at the ceiling, gesturing towards the lawless world above. "Where I come from? Up there?" She clicked her teeth. "Honor just gets you killed."

eighteen

"Would you mind if I brought Teir in here to continue our discussion?" Rafa asked Sadie.

Sadie managed to sit up in bed, grimacing the whole way.

"Where does it hurt?" Rafa asked.

"Not so much hurt, more like ache. Like a bad hangover." A thought then hit her. "You know what a hangover is? You got stuff like whiskey down here? Bug spit or something?"

Rafa smiled politely and went to touch her forehead. Sadie, no longer as weak as she'd been when she'd woken from her state, flinched. Rafa's hand recoiled slightly, his polite smile becoming a reassuring one as he kept his arm extended. Sadie sighed, her wariness of Rafa's touch visibly deflating as she exhaled, and Rafa ultimately placed his hand on her brow.

"Your fever is down," he said. "You're a fast healer."

"I have a feeling I have you to thank for that," she said. "What have you been treating me with?"

"I can show you in time; you've still much healing to do. Getting back to Teir..."

"I'm not getting in the kid's head again," she said firmly. "If you wanna know what I saw in there, I'll tell you, and then *you* can decide how best to discuss it with him, but I'm not letting the kid see what *I* saw. Crazy as it sounds, it was probably a good thing it happened to him so

ing when our memories can only hold so much. Not to mention his
.sion had just started to go." She smiled without a trace of humor. "Talk
about your twisted examples of irony."

"Another admirable quality in you," Rafa said. "You wish to protect
Teir."

"I wish to protect my investment. I want him to take me to the tunnel. If I got into his head again and he saw those memories with my eyes,
who knows what'll happen? He won't be good to any of us if he loses his
shit."

"I had no intention of delving into the memories you released in Teir
so soon. The purpose for my suggesting Teir join us now is to ask him
about this tunnel. Teir and I have very few secrets."

"Everybody's got secrets," Sadie said. "I wouldn't let it bother you."

"I'm not offended, only curious. I'd like to get the truth directly from
him."

Sadie considered it. She had questions for the kid too. Quite a few.
Having someone like Rafa acting as mediator could only help in getting
more than grunts and nods from the headstrong bugger who was assuredly still bitter from their last interaction.

"Okay," Sadie said. "Bring him on in."

. . .

The three of them were back together in the room: Sadie still propped up
in bed; Rafa the caregiver still by her side; and Teir back to his wary vigil
by the foot of the bed.

Rafa apparently chose to forgo small talk and get right to the point.
Sadie was pleased. According to her, in a time when the life expectancy
was forty, small talk and futility were one and the same.

"Tell us about the tunnel, Teir," Rafa asked.

And Teir did. Hesitant and cryptic at first, perhaps for what Rafa
might think of his deception, perhaps the teenager in him punishing
Sadie from their last encounter, but ultimately his story was told, and told
in full.

And now it was Sadie's turn.

She was curt, her story playing out more like notes than a tale, using
her gift for cheating in cards like she always did. Except she took it too far

this time, despite knowing it would bring trouble. And it did. Her identity as a martyr had been blown. Two dead by her hand. One a member of the infamous Blue. They would want vengeance. More so, the Blue warlord would insist on abducting her first, torturing her until she agreed to utilize her gift in locating endless pockets of Clear, wringing her body dry until the extremities of sickness made death a favor.

As for her dreams? Teir's involvement in it all? Sadie explained she felt it was all fairly obvious. Teir's solo adventures throughout his community had led him to a hidden tunnel that Sadie believed led below the Blue compound. Sadie's visions of Russian roulette and a revolver packed with blue bullets were telling her that she'd made her bed and it was only a matter of time until one of those blue bullets found their way between her eyes, *unless* she heeded Teir's advice and followed the tunnel beneath the compound and killed the Blue warlord before he and his people had a chance to kill her first.

"But that *wasn't* Teir's implication in the dream," Rafa broke in. "How could it have been?"

"Because I'm a martyr," Sadie said flatly. "I see shit."

Rafa shook his head, looking agitated. "Teir had no prior knowledge of where the tunnel led to *or* your troubles with this Blue gang."

Sadie splayed her hands. "I'm open to interpretation."

"You claim you don't ordinarily cheat very long in card games for fear of being found out a martyr, correct?"

"Correct."

"Yet this time with the Blue gang member, you did. You were risking your identity *and* your life."

"Correct again."

"At first, you didn't know why you did it; you said so yourself just now."

Sadie nodded, beginning to look bored.

"But then an epiphany hit you before you passed out on the side of the road, yes? Before Teir found you?"

"I wouldn't call it an epiphany—more like the acceptance of a sad truth."

Rafa seemed undeterred by her pessimistic need for distinction. "And that sad truth was?"

Sadie studied Rafa for a beat. Wily as they came, Sadie had to admit she had no clue where this guy was headed with his questioning. She accommodated him anyway. "The sad truth is that there *is* no utopia. Only the here and now. Either you accept that…or you succumb to hope."

"Well, then perhaps *that's* what led you here," Rafa said. "Not to carry out some pre-emptive strike on a warlord. Perhaps you're with us for that 'here and now'…for that chance at a life."

"As a *mole*?"

"If this tunnel does lead you beneath the Blue gang's compound—and we still don't know if it does—and you carry out your plan of executing this warlord, what then? What will you do then?"

Sadie raised an eyebrow as though the answer was evident. "I'll stop worrying about being hunted."

"And your identity as a martyr?" Rafa said. "You claimed there were dozens of witnesses in the tavern that day. How soon until word spreads to other gangs, other warlords?"

"You're suggesting I hide below ground with you people? I'm not the hiding type."

"But isn't that what you've been doing all this time? Hiding in plain sight? As a martyr? How nice would it be to not carry that burden around anymore? The constant fear of people finding out your identity? How nice to live in a community with people who would know and accept and not exploit your gift?"

Sadie laughed. "*Exploit?* You want to use my gift to help you find Clear!"

"As part of an *agreement.* You struck a deal with Teir, did you not? Besides, I'm now offering a better deal, right here, right now." Rafa leaned in. "Forget this silliness with the Blue gang. Live with us here, where you will be safe. Use your gift to mine Clear for us. When your sickness follows, I will personally nurse you back to health."

Sadie said nothing.

Rafa went on. "In exchange for utilizing your gift and providing our community with Clear, you will have a chance at an existence where hope is something to be cherished and not feared."

Sadie remained quiet.

"You've already admitted you'd practically given up, Sadie," Rafa continued. "Your act at the tavern with the Blue gang member was akin to suicide." He splayed his hands, his proposal coming to a close. "We're offering you a second chance at life. A *real* life." Rafa stood, brought his hands together in conclusion. "Don't answer now. When you're better, I can show you around the community myself to help you in your decision. Does that sound fair?"

Sadie shrugged. "Sure." She glanced over at Teir. "What do you think, kiddo? Think you'd like having me stay here?"

"Sure thing, princess."

Rafa started chuckling. "Let's go, Teir."

Sadie frowned. "I miss the joke?"

Teir left.

Just the two of them now, Rafa said: "Teir asked one of our librarians to research the meaning of your name due to your insistence upon calling him 'kiddo.' He was pleased to learn that Sadie means 'princess.'"

Sadie smirked. "Oh, well, isn't he a spiteful little one."

"Please think about my offer." Rafa turned to leave.

"Rafa?"

He stopped at the door.

"I told you before; I'm still not a hundred percent sure how this damn 'gift' works. As soon as I think I've got it figured out, it laughs in my face."

Rafa nodded. "I understand. I'm sure that—"

"No, you don't understand," Sadie said, cutting him off. "I'm not a hundred percent sure, but I am painfully familiar with a lot of it. And here's something I *do* know. The things I sometimes see? They haven't happened yet. You following me?"

Rafa took a step away from the door, closer to Sadie. "I'm not sure I am."

"That dream I had about Teir? The one where he brought me to the tunnel to help me kill the Blue warlord?"

"I already told you your interpretation of that dream was flawed."

Sadie shrugged. "Maybe it was. Or maybe it just hasn't happened yet."

nineteen

General Gash sat in his throne, thrumming his thick fingers on the arm-rest as he waited for Wrath, his number one, to return. Gash's quarters sat high atop the Blue compound where he was able to keep an eye on his men at all times through the lenses of powerful telescopes he'd tortured countless nomads to obtain.

At General Gash's feet, shackled young men massaged his calves. By his head, young women kneaded his broad shoulders. One of the women was visibly showing with Gash's child. The bump repulsed him. As soon as the child was born, he would cast the woman off into the wastelands to die of attrition as he'd done with all the others. If the child was a female, she would join her mother.

General Gash reached forward and snatched the scalp of one of the young men at his feet, jerking him upright. "Gin," he said to the boy.

The young man nodded and hobbled away as fast as he could in the iron clutching his ankles. While the boy busied himself in the corner of the chamber preparing the general his drink behind the vast bar that con-tained the finest of alcohols obtainable in the wastelands, Gash gripped one of the young women by the neck and pulled her towards him. "I'll have you tonight," he said. He pulled her in closer, sniffed her up and down as an animal would, then traced his thick tongue along her neck and cheek. Her smell was ripe; her taste, salty and sour. "You'll bathe first."

He shoved her away. The woman looked grateful—not for the encounter to come with Gash, but for the opportunity to bathe.

"Bathe her," Gash called to one of his men standing guard by his door. "Bathe her and *only* bathe her. She's to be mine and mine alone."

The gang member nodded and took the young woman away. The boy approached with the general's sizeable cup of gin, lost his footing in the shackle's unforgiving grasp, and tumbled forward, spilling the drink at the feet of General Gash.

Gash's quarters, despite their isolated location at the very top of the compound, were typically buzzing with at least some type of ambient sound—engines of motorhorses circling the perimeter of the compound in the distance; gang members carrying on below with drink and cards and brutality. Now it was as if everyone and everything in the compound had incredulously witnessed the event unfolding at General Gash's feet; the silence was sudden and breathtaking, laden with horrific anticipation.

The young man did not bother to get to his feet. He lay sprawled out on the chamber floor, as if knowing to rise and beg was futile.

"Stand," General Gash told the boy.

The young man stood. So did Gash. He circled the boy, considering him. The boy was all of seventeen, frail and weak, clad in nothing but a loincloth. General Gash, short but powerful, was adorned in quality cloth and leather, animal skins, and chains. His heavily tanned face was an ideal canvas for the crisscrossing lines of white scars that ran as high as the scalp of his thinning black hair, all the way down to his neck, one line in particular slicing through his right eye en route, leaving the eye long since dead and discolored. Gash did not hide this truth with a patch as others might—chose instead to wield it as a visual reminder to those who dared challenge him, a reminder of what he'd endured, how hard he was to kill. One might even say Gash's choice to display the dead eye was to provide stark contrast to its working neighbor, heightening that neighbor's intensity, showcasing a dark and pitiless window to a soul that didn't exist.

General Gash now stood behind the young man. Twice the boy's width, he placed both powerful hands on the boy's scrawny shoulders and began to massage them gently. The young man's head hung the entire time: no tears, no pleas, still resigned to his fate whatever it may be.

"If I remove your hands," Gash began softly into the nape of the boy's neck, "then you would no longer be able to carry my drinks."

The boy said nothing.

"If I remove your feet," Gash continued, "then you would no longer be able to *bring* me my drinks." Gash then chuckled. "Though even fully intact, you seem incapable of such a task."

The two gang members guarding the door snorted at their general's remark. Gash glanced over at them. His expression was enough to drop their smiles instantly. They spun back to their positions on the door, postures overly vigilant.

Gash began massaging the boy's shoulders again. "What to do… what to do…"

There was a knock at the door. One of the guards slid back the steel cover to the rectangular peephole and checked. He then turned over his shoulder to General Gash. "It's Wrath."

"Let him in then, fool," Gash said.

Wrath, General Gash's number one, entered. Tall and thin with wiry muscle that showed in his arms through the sleeveless leather jacket he wore, Wrath approached his general.

Gash continued massaging the boy's shoulders as he spoke. "Well?"

"Not much," Wrath said. Wrath's speech was affected by the fact that he had no front teeth. Abducted by a rival gang years back, Wrath was tortured for days, his front teeth removed with pliers. Wrath had since obtained his revenge, removing the gang's former warlord's front teeth himself. He now wore those same teeth around his neck, along with a host of others. Wrath currently had twenty-eight front teeth hanging around his neck and was always eager to add more.

"Couple of folks at that watering hole about twelve miles up claim they saw them drinking and talking with Finn," Wrath continued. "They claim they all left on their own, though—Finn first, then our boys an hour or so later."

Gash looked away in thought. To the newly arrived, it might have appeared that massaging the boy's shoulders helped him think.

Wrath certainly spotted it. "What's this about?" he asked, gesturing to them both.

Gash broke from his train of thought, turned his head towards Wrath. "Spilled my gin," he replied casually. "Trying to figure out how to handle it."

Wrath gestured with his necklace, his green, almost reptilian eyes asking his general's permission.

"Maybe," Gash said, looking away in thought again. He spoke his thoughts aloud as though dictating a letter. "Rumor is strong that Finn and Vidar still keep in touch."

"Finn's a bounty hunter now," Wrath said. "Money's all that matters to him to these days."

Gash broke his gaze and placed it back on Wrath again. "Are you forgetting when he alone claimed three of ours after Sten's death? I'm still not sure who was who, he carved them up so bad."

"I got my licks in," Wrath said.

"You couldn't finish the job."

Wrath's upper lip curled in a flash of disgust as he fingered a sizeable scar along the side of his neck. "Neither could he."

A sly smirk creased the corner of Gash's mouth. He enjoyed riling up his number one about the only man who'd crossed him and lived. Gash knew Wrath would toss all twenty-eight teeth around his neck if he could have Finn's two.

Wrath shook it off and added: "Finn and me tangled years ago, General. Why would he wait so long to mount another attack?"

"Vidar," was all Gash said.

"Vidar hasn't come after us in a while, either. Same question: Why wait so long?"

"Because I murdered his family, Wrath," he replied casually. "Something like that has no time limit." General Gash suddenly clamped onto the boy's head and wrenched it to one side, snapping his neck and killing him instantly. The boy dropped to the floor like dead meat.

"Go on, then," Gash said to Wrath, gesturing to his necklace. "Be quick about it."

Wrath grinned his toothless grin, withdrew the pliers he carried with him everywhere, and bent to collect his prize.

·   ·   ·

"Okay," Wrath said, standing up and wiping his pliers on his pants before tucking teeth twenty-nine and thirty into his breast pocket. "So what's your theory then?"

General Gash sat back down in his throne, the remaining boy immediately massaging his legs as though he'd witnessed nothing; the two young women at his head continuing on his shoulders as if they too were blind to it all.

"This recent martyr business? Gunning down one of ours in cold blood?" Gash said. "Perhaps there's a connection somewhere."

"Like what?"

"I gave the order to hold off on the hunt for the martyr, didn't I?"

Wrath nodded.

"Perhaps two of our boys took it upon themselves to seek her out anyway. Get in my good graces should they find her sooner than later."

"So they go to *Finn* to help find her?" Wrath asked.

"Maybe. Everyone knows how good Finn is. Perhaps our boys assumed as you did, thought Finn only cared about money."

"So then what? Finn kills them? Just like that?"

"Maybe he brings them to Vidar instead—happily." Gash clenched his massive fist.

Wrath digested it all for a moment. "Still think the martyr's in hiding? Still wanna hold off on the hunt?"

Gash nodded. "She'd have to be crazy to show her face so soon."

twenty

Teir paced Rafa's small office in the clinic as they waited for Sadie to finish showering and get into some clean clothes.

"What's taking her so long?" Teir muttered.

Rafa didn't answer right away. Teir knew Rafa was worried about him—even more worried than usual—but he couldn't bring himself to care about anything except not giving in to the rage and grief that were trying to swallow him.

"It's likely she's never bathed in such a well-equipped facility in her life," Rafa finally said. "Let alone one in which she feels reasonably safe. Who could blame her for taking her time?"

Teir stopped pacing, took a deep breath in through his nose and exhaled slowly out his mouth, just as Rafa had taught him, to try to calm himself down. He did this three times.

It did no good. Scenes of shadowy, blood-drenched horror seared his mind.

And the screams of his dying mother.

And the laughter of the men making her scream.

He swallowed hard, clenched his fists and jaw, and vowed for what had to be the thousandth time that somehow he would find those laughing men and make them very, *very* sorry for what they had done.

The sound of Sadie's voice jolted him back to the present, and immediately a different sort of rage swept through him. "It's about time," he said under his breath.

Rafa stood from his desk chair as Sadie entered the room. "Ready for a short tour of the community?" he asked.

She chuckled. "Ready as I'll ever be."

.   .   .

Teir stayed close to Rafa's side as they showed Sadie around a few of the main common areas. He'd forced himself to drink a protein shake a few hours ago, but only so Elixa would stop begging him to eat something. He couldn't remember how many hours it had been since he'd slept. Though he'd dozed off a few times in the chair at the foot of Sadie's bed, all it did was allow the gruesome scenes of his mother's murder to run more freely through his head. Now, with those scenes still consuming his thoughts, he was so exhausted it was all he could do to put one foot in front of the other, let alone navigate the community's dim hallways himself.

He resisted the urge to slip his hand around Rafa's arm as they moved along. He didn't want Rafa to be any more worried about him than he already was, and he definitely didn't want Sadie to think he needed anyone's help to get around. Instead, he concentrated on the sound of Rafa's voice as his friend played tour guide. Teir's earliest memories of feeling comfortable and safe were narrated by Rafa, and his voice still had the power to keep Teir calm and focused like nothing else.

When Sadie did comment or ask a question, it broke Teir's concentration. Once it caused him to stumble, and he grabbed the back of Rafa's jacket to steady himself. The next time his concentration was broken, he nearly fell to his knees before he grabbed Rafa's arm and regained his footing.

"Sadie, you must be hungry," Rafa said. "My apologies for not offering you a proper meal right away. My eagerness to show off our community caused me to take leave of my manners. Please forgive me."

Teir heard her chuckle softly. "My stomach hasn't exactly been up for eating the past day or so, but thanks to your talents I think maybe I could actually eat now." She paused. "Though if what I've heard about your eating habits are true, you'll have to forgive me for my lack of enthusiasm about your cuisine."

Rafa led them to D Caff, their favorite cafe. Teir had no idea what time it was, but he guessed it was late in the evening because the place was nearly empty, for which he was ridiculously grateful. It was bad enough that Sadie would see how stress and lack of sleep made his hands shake; at least he didn't have to feel like the whole room was watching him too.

They approached the counter, and Teir ordered cricket bars, both with extra jumil paste.

"*Cricket bars?*" Sadie said.

"They're very flavorful and nutritious," Rafa told her. "And they're made from cricket flour, so they don't appear at all to be made from insects. I was going to suggest you give them a try, to ease you into entomophagy."

"Ento-what?"

"Entomophagy," Rafa repeated. "The practice of eating insects. The word derives from the Greek terms *éntomos* or *éntomon*, literally meaning 'cut in two,' referring to an insect's segmented body, and *phăgein*, which means 'to eat.'"

"You don't have any animal meat?" she asked.

"It is possible to obtain dried and occasionally fresh animal meats from some of the nomadic tribes with whom we trade," Rafa explained, "but it's very costly and unhealthy. The majority of our community members practice entomophagy. We farm dozens of species in meticulously sanitary conditions, and they're prepared for consumption in a wide variety of ways by culinary experts."

"You want me to eat *bugs*."

There was an uncomfortable pause.

Then Rafa spoke. "Yes. Please. Just try them."

Sadie sighed. "Okay. Then I guess I'll have some cricket bars," she said. "What's jumil paste?"

"It tastes gross," Teir mumbled. "You won't like it."

"So why'd you get it?" she asked.

"To save Rafa the trouble of convincing me to eat it because it's good for me."

Rafa ordered cricket bars for Sadie and himself, and beverages for the three of them. They then brought their food to a booth. Teir took a few steadying breaths before he began his meal, but it did no good. His tremors were as bad as ever.

Of course Sadie had to say something. "You okay, kiddo?"

Teir snapped: "Spectacular, princess. How are your bugs? Warn us if you're gonna puke, okay?"

"Whoa, take it easy," she said. "I'm not giving you shit. I'm concerned. Your hands are shaking like fish out of water."

Teir's brain took a quick detour as he tried to remember what a fish was, and Rafa took the opportunity to explain Teir's tremors as only Rafa could. "The postural tremors are a minor neurologic abnormality common in individuals with the type of bilateral optic neuropathy that affects his vision. They're exacerbated by physical and psychological fatigue."

"Okaaay…" she said. "I appreciate you not dumbing things down for me, but the science talk is way over my head. Try again in words I might actually understand."

"The wire that runs from my eyes to my brain is defective," Teir broke in. "In some people with this condition, it also makes your hands shake, especially when you're tired or stressed out."

"Is it a disease?"

"No. It's genetic," Rafa told her

"Someone in my family had it," Teir added.

"Who?" she asked.

Teir had a sudden urge to shout that if she really wanted to know, she should crawl inside his head again so they could both get some answers, but he managed to control himself. It seemed the jumiles really did calm him down. He took another bite of a cricket bar, held back a grimace at the bitterness of the jumiles, then chewed and swallowed before he answered her. "All I know about my family is what you showed me about my mother. I don't even know my name."

"Your name is Teiresias," Rafa said quietly.

Teir felt a stab of guilt at the sadness in his friend's voice. "And I've had this name longer than I had the other one, but I'd still like to know what it was."

They finished their meal in silence.

.   .   .

"The bugs weren't as disgusting as I thought they'd be," Sadie admitted.

"That's positive...correct?" Rafa asked.

"It means I won't starve while I'm here, so yes, I'd say it's positive."

Rafa began to tell her about the various types of insects they ate, how they were farmed and prepared, and of course how nutritious they were. This led to talk about other features of the community that he hadn't yet covered, like how it was run by an elected committee, the importance of art and culture in keeping things civilized, the huge amount of information they had in their library, and the sustainable technologies that kept the air and water clean and the electricity flowing.

Sadie shared a few stories of her own, mostly about the world above and its *lack* of civilization, technology, and culture.

Teir kept his eyes open for as long as he could before finally giving in to the urge to rest them.

Eventually, the brutal scenes that had been tormenting him fell silent and faded to black.

twenty-one

"Is he asleep?" Rafa asked.

"Sure looks like it," Sadie told him. "Poor kid. He's had a hellish couple of days."

"He's had a hellish life," Rafa corrected her.

Rafa watched Sadie study them from across the tabletop, her gaze moving from him to Teir and back. "From what I saw when I was in his head, the past few years have been pretty good," she said. "How long has he lived in your community?"

"Eight years."

"And who found him?"

"I did."

It was now Rafa's turn to study Sadie. Did she know the circumstances in which Teir was found? Had she witnessed this in her travels through his mind? Of course Teir himself had no memory of it, given the grave condition in which he was discovered, but once the boy had reached an age at which Rafa deemed him able to handle the information, he had spared no details in relating it to him. It was an unpleasant story, but it was the only story Teir had about his origins, and Rafa felt he had a right to know it.

Rafa's own mind flashed back to the moment he'd found the boy—the skeletal body, so small and vulnerable, skin blistered by the sun and bruised by the hands of the monsters who'd put him in an iron collar and shackles. Rafa forced himself back to the present, taking great comfort in the fact that the child he'd discovered close to death beneath a bush was now the healthy and intelligent adolescent who was slumped against him napping.

"Any idea how old he is?" she asked.

"We recently celebrated his fourteenth birthday. Obviously his age is a guess, but I believe it's close to accurate."

"Who here raised him?"

"My grandmother helped, as did my sister, Izar, but I've always been his primary caretaker."

Sadie's eyes widened. "You? You're only a kid yourself."

"I'm twenty."

"Which would've made you, what, *twelve* when you found him?"

Rafa nodded.

"Where's your mother?" she asked.

It had been a very long time since Rafa had met someone who was unaware of his mother's fate and of her son's crippling sorrow in its wake. He was shocked by his sudden willingness—no, *desire*—to reveal his darkest secret to this stranger. Perhaps her martyr gift did exert some influence on him after all.

Or perhaps it was just that the time had finally come to unburden himself.

"Six months before I found Teir, an aggressive illness took my mother's life," he told her. "We'd been extremely close. I was lost without her." He stared at the tabletop, unable to meet Sadie's gaze. "I'd removed a vial of serum from my grandmother's pharmacy that I knew to be lethal in high doses." He glanced at Teir sleeping peacefully beside him. "But when I found him, my world completely shifted its focus. Saving his life and caring for him became far more important than escaping my grief."

"What a waste that would have been," she said.

"Yes. The serum is a powerful remedy for several life-threatening conditions and very difficult to obtain."

"Wait—*what?*" Her tone demanded his attention, and he forced himself to meet her gaze. "You're not kidding, are you? You really *do* think that little of yourself." She shook her head. "Sad."

He lowered his gaze back to the tabletop.

Sadie went on. "Your little friend here has more self-respect in his toenail than you have in that great big brain of yours," she said. "Obviously he didn't learn it from you."

Rafa kept quiet.

"I haven't survived this long by being a bad judge of character, and I don't need to crawl inside your head to know that your gifts are as rare and valuable as mine." She sat back and crossed her arms in front of her. "In fact, given your gifts, I wonder how it is you haven't figured out a cure for Cling that doesn't require *my* gifts."

He opened his mouth to share his current theories culled from his obsessive research on the topic, but she raised a hand and halted his words.

"Don't," she said. "Please. More science talk will put me over the edge right now." She gestured at Teir. "Let's get this kid home and into his own bed."

. . .

Rafa returned to the living room after getting Teir bedded down and back to sleep. Sadie had removed her boots, stretched out on the couch and pulled the throw blanket over herself.

"This is some bachelor pad you've got here," she said. "I like the open floor plan. I guess when you live underground, the less walls the better, huh? Are all the apartments this nice?"

"As I explained during our tour earlier, the facility was equipped with state-of-the-art amenities and furnishings when it was constructed, and although it's now quite old, it's been well cared for. That goes for the residential units as well. This is actually one of the smaller apartments. There are some that can accommodate large extended families very comfortably."

"It's so *clean*. Especially considering there are two young guys living here."

Rafa smiled. "I keep it tidy so Teir doesn't have to navigate an obstacle course of debris." He stepped into the kitchen area and poured himself a cup of water. "Can I offer you anything to eat or drink?"

"Some water would be nice."

He poured her a cup and brought it to her. She thanked him, drank the whole cup in a few gulps, handed it back to him, and reclined again, pulling the blanket up to her chin.

"Are you sure you're all right staying with us?" he asked. "My grandmother said you're welcome to stay with her at the clinic, and my sister also opened her home to you. She and her husband and daughter live in a much larger unit. They even have a guest room."

"In my wildest dreams, I can't imagine anywhere I'd rather sleep right now than this freakishly comfortable couch."

He smiled. "I'll be just down the hall should you need anything."

twenty-two

Rafa woke the next morning to find Teir still sound asleep. The boy had slept through the night for the first time in months. In the dim light, Rafa watched the rhythmic rise and fall of his chest, relieved to see his youthful visage minus the stress and sorrow of the past few days.

He found Sadie awake in the living room. She stood examining the world map on the wall, her fingers gliding over the tactile borders that facilitated Teir's ability to study its geography. He crossed the room to stand beside her.

"You made this for him?" she asked.

"Yes."

"Why?"

"An insular existence should not preclude an understanding of the larger picture."

"I bet you know all about what it was like before it went to hell."

"I've read extensively about it."

She continued her study of the map in silence for a moment, then asked: "Where'd the big rock that caused the Event land?"

He placed his finger on the map in the middle of the largest ocean.

"I bet you know all about that, too," she said.

"I do. I'll tell you about it if you like."

She flashed him a sardonic smirk, then turned away, shaking her head. "Hell no."

"How are you feeling today?" he asked.

"A little fuzzy, but rested."

"You slept well?"

"Like a baby."

"Are you hungry?"

She turned back to him. "Are you gonna feed me bugs again?"

"Yes."

She rolled her eyes, her smirk much less sardonic. "Fine."

.   .   .

Rafa was cleaning up from breakfast when there was a knock at the door. A peek through the door's small viewing hole revealed an unwelcome sight. He closed his eyes and rested his forehead against the cool metal door for a few breaths. He then stepped back and opened it.

"Good morning, Julen," he said.

"Son," was the curt response as his father stepped into the apartment uninvited and crossed the floor to where Sadie stood in the kitchen area. He extended his hand to her. "Julen Carrera, Rafael's father."

She shook his hand. "Sadie."

"On behalf of our entire community, I welcome you, Sadie. Our governing committee will convene at eleven hours to formally greet you, express our collective gratitude, and apprise you of our strategy for a mutually beneficial relationship, after which a banquet brunch will be held with you as our honored guest."

Sadie's eyes narrowed. She shot Rafa a withering glare over Julen's shoulder. Rafa's heart began to race, and he felt himself break into a cold sweat beneath the weight of her silent accusation. Her words echoed in his mind:

Me and the kid had a deal. He gets me to the tunnel, I find you guys some Clear.

Julen turned to face his son. "See that she is appropriately attired and escort her to North Hall."

Rafa took a deep breath and exhaled softly.

Julen excused himself and headed for the door, then added: "And leave the boy here."

Rafa swallowed the lump in his throat and willed his voice not to waver. "No."

His father turned quickly. "Rafael, I will *not* have him at a committee meeting, and the banquet is a formal event for adults only."

"Teir is the one who found her," Rafa said.

"By *accident*, due to reckless behavior for which he most definitely should *not* be rewarded."

Rafa felt himself gaining momentum and hoped the ground would not slide out from beneath him. "It was not by accident. He smelled the gasoline from her machine and followed the scent."

"And if the scent had led him to a pack of bloodthirsty gang members instead of an ailing woman, he would have gotten himself and possibly your entire expedition killed when you heard his screams and ran to his rescue!"

Rafa clenched his fists as his vision swam and his heart pounded against the inside of his chest. "He did not put anyone at risk, including himself, because he is perceptive and intelligent. But that's not the point. Teir is not going to the meeting or the banquet, nor are Sadie and I."

Julen closed the short distance between them. "*What?*"

"Teir and Sadie made a deal that is exclusively between the two of them. It is not the business of the committee or anyone else. She has promised to obtain Clear for us as part of this deal, and it is for her to decide thereafter if she wishes to meet the committee or remain in the community. Today Teir will fulfill his part of the deal to Sadie, and if anyone interferes they will jeopardize Sadie's benevolence and, by extension, the health of us all."

His father had never threatened him with violence, but the man's enraged expression now hinted at the very real possibility. Instead, Julen turned and walked out of the apartment without another word.

Rafa ran to the bathroom, dropped to his knees in front of the toilet, and vomited.

twenty-three

Teir leapt out of bed and hurried down the hall to the bathroom to find Rafa sitting on the floor with his back against the side of the tub.

"Rafa? Are you okay?"

"Yes."

Teir wasn't convinced. He grabbed a washcloth, wet it under the sink faucet, and handed it to Rafa. While Rafa wiped his face with the damp cloth, Teir brought him a cup of water from the kitchen. Rafa swished the first gulp around in his mouth and spit it into the toilet, then drank the rest.

"Thanks," Rafa said quietly.

"Come on, I'll help you up."

Rafa took Teir's extended hand and let himself be pulled to his feet.

"You wanna lay down?" Teir asked him.

"No."

Teir followed him into the living room where they joined Sadie. Rafa lowered himself onto the couch, and Teir sat down beside him and tried his best to unravel his conflicting emotions after what he'd just overheard and witnessed—sheer joy that Rafa had stood up to his high-and-mighty father for once, and sorrow that it had made him lose his breakfast.

Sadie broke the silence. "Your old man's sure wound pretty tight."

"Sorry about that," Rafa said. "He's just doing what he believes is best."

"Whatever." Sadie stood and gave Teir's foot a nudge with her own. "Come on, kiddo; get your ass in gear. We've got a tunnel to explore."

.   .   .

Teir quickly fed himself, showered and dressed.

The haunting images that had tormented him the past couple days were still lurking in the back of his mind, and he was still angry that Sadie had refused to help him see more, but after such a good night's rest—the first he'd had in a long time—he found it much easier to focus his thoughts on more positive things, like that Sadie was going to help their community so Rafa wouldn't have to work himself half to death trying to find a cure for Cling.

He'd just rejoined Rafa and Sadie in the living room when there was a knock at the door.

"I'll answer it," he told them as he stood and crossed the room. The viewing hole useless to him, Teir spoke to the closed door. "Who is it?"

"Izar," came the response from the other side.

Teir opened the door for her. She entered and gave him a kiss on the cheek, then greeted Rafa and Sadie.

Izar's self-confidence and determination had always impressed Teir, and of course he admired her combat skills and physical strength. Although he adored Rafa, he wished his friend was more like his sister in these ways and often wondered how the pair had been raised by the same parents but turned out so different from each other.

"*Rafaelito*," Izar said quietly. "*Hablemos.*"

Rafa followed her into the far corner of the room where they began speaking in their family's common language at a volume Teir could barely hear.

"What are they saying?" Sadie asked.

Teir listened carefully, bristling at what he could understand. "She's telling him what their father said about the scene here a little while ago."

"How the hell did this suddenly become a family drama?"

"It's okay," Teir said. "She's not here to give Rafa grief. Even though Julen sent her, she'll probably take Rafa's side once she hears what he has to say. Don't be surprised if she ends up coming with us to the tunnel."

Sure enough, when they rejoined Teir and Sadie in the sitting area, Rafa simply said: "Izar will be joining us today."

"How nice," Sadie muttered.

"Hopefully we won't run into trouble," Izar said. "But if we do, although Teir is a very good fighter, he's at a great disadvantage in very low light. And Rafa is not a fighter at all."

Teir tugged on Izar's sleeve. "Which pistol did you bring?"

"The Beretta."

"Really?" Sadie said with genuine interest. "You got good bullets?"

"I've got two ten-round .45 ACP cartridges with me," Izar told her.

"You sure they're good?" Sadie reiterated.

"I'm not sure I follow," Izar said.

"Good—*real*—bullets aren't easy to come by above ground. They're kinda like Clear that way—you can take your chances buying from nomads or peddlers, but nine times out of ten, you're getting a shoddy product. Of course you only realize this when it's too late. End up paying with both your money and your life."

"*You* have real bullets," Rafa said.

"I get mine the same way I'm gonna get you your Clear. It's not fun, but it's reliable. Only other way is through a legitimate arms dealer, and those people don't exactly advertise."

Izar brandished the gun. "I assure you, these bullets are real. I filled the shells myself."

"Tedious work."

"Yes, it is, but much like you utilizing your gift to locate real bullets, it is reliable."

Sadie smiled. "I thought you people were pacifists."

"Most in the community are," Izar said. "But not me. It's my job to defend my people." She brandished the gun again. "I'm willing to die for them."

"Works for me," Sadie said. "Shall we go?"

Teir led them to the remote part of the complex that was used for storing supplies. They passed several people on the way who greeted Izar, as she was well-liked throughout the community, but she did no more than briefly return the greeting and keep moving. No one followed them, and, as usual, there was no one around in the storage area.

Teir brought them to the door with "N-6" painted on it in bold black letters, gave the handle a tug, opened it, and stood back.

"It's full of boxes and old junk," he told them, "but behind all that is the tunnel."

"How long is it?" Izar asked.

"I don't know. I've never made it to the end."

"How far *have* you made it?" Sadie asked.

"To the white *X* I drew on the wall."

"Why did you draw the *X*?" Rafa asked.

It dawned on Teir that no one had asked him that question yet, not even Sadie. The truth would make him sound crazy to just about anyone, but given what Sadie had told them about her dream-vision in which Teir had brought her to the tunnel and shown her the *X* drawn in blue, and her theories on what it all meant, maybe it wasn't so crazy after all.

"Because I heard voices."

twenty-four

"*Voices?*" Izar said.

Teir nodded.

"Maybe it was just your own people back in the community," Sadie said. "Things echo down here."

"Do you hear anything now?" Teir asked.

Everyone went quiet for a moment.

"Hear anything?" Teir asked again.

They all shook their heads.

"If you don't hear our people out here, no *way* are you gonna hear them all the way in there—" He gestured into the depths of the tunnel.

The kid was right, Sadie thought. It had to be someone else. And if her gut and premonitions were any indicator as to whom those *someone elses* might be...

"Okay," Sadie said, turning and facing the group. "Gimme the flashlights."

"Rowlights," Teir said.

"Whatever. Let me have them."

"You're going in alone?" Rafa asked.

"Yup. Gimme the lights."

"I should go with you," Izar said, raising the Beretta to underline her reasoning.

"Your job is to protect your people, not me. You said so yourself."

"I'm not sure it's wise to go in alone," Rafa said.

"I go alone or no Clear."

A moment of pause.

"If this tunnel does lead to the Blue compound somehow, what will you do?" Rafa asked.

"I already told you what I was going to do."

"And you plan to do that *now*? Are you even familiar with the layout of this Blue compound? Where the warlord resides within? How many guards? Where—?"

"Slow down, stress ball. Right now I'm all about following this tunnel until it ends."

"And if the Blue compound *is* at the end?" Izar reiterated.

"Then I do exactly as Rafa suggests and get the layout of the place."

"So you *do* plan to go up now," Izar said.

"Not exactly."

Another brief pause before Rafa said: "You plan to utilize your gift."

Sadie touched the tip of her nose. "I'll get it all—how many gang members; where they're stationed; where the warlord resides; and, most importantly, as many above-ground exit points as possible."

"Above-ground exit points?" Rafa said. "You don't plan to return to us after you've eliminated your threat?"

"Whether I do or don't is irrelevant—the second I head up there to kill the son of a bitch, you're gonna be bricking up this tunnel so that no one can get through here again."

"What?" Teir said.

Sadie took a deep breath. "If I go up there and get killed and they eventually find out how I infiltrated their compound, you don't think they'll file on down here and tear this place apart?"

"And if you go up there and *do* succeed in killing the warlord, won't his men file on down here all the same in pursuit of vengeance?" Izar asked.

Sadie shook her head. "These gangs are aimless fools without a leader. There's a hierarchy among them, but it's about as sturdy as a drunk in a sandstorm. They won't be focused on vengeance; their greed will preoccupy them with aspirations of power. Hell, some will even be grateful their warlord is dead."

Nobody responded.

"So are we clear then?" Sadie asked. "Once I'm up there, I'm up there. No going back down the way I came."

"How could we do such a job so quickly?" Rafa asked. "Bricking up the tunnel? It's at *least* a solid day's work."

"You'll start before I even head up. Leave just enough room in the wall for me to squeeze through and then plug that hole forever once I'm on the other side."

"Then what?" Teir asked.

"Then you wish me luck, kiddo."

Izar turned to Rafa. "Perhaps we should start now. Begin gathering supplies for the wall."

"Wait until I get back," Sadie said. "No point starting to build a wall if the tunnel ends up leading nowhere."

"What if you get sick?" Rafa asked.

"What?"

"At the end of the tunnel. Utilizing your gift to obtain the layout of the compound?"

"I *will* get sick," she said. "But not like before. Besides, you'll make me well again, right?" She smiled and gave Rafa a friendly little punch on the shoulder.

Rafa only nodded in return. "Of course I will."

"And don't worry," Sadie said to the group, "I haven't forgotten our deal. When I return, we'll begin our search for your Clear."

"When you're well enough," Rafa said.

Sadie nodded and felt the kindness of these people threaten her rule against forming bonds for the risk it posed, against ignoring the gut for matters of the heart.

"Gimme the flashlights," she said. "I'll be back when I'm back."

twenty-five

The kid was right. The tunnel did go on forever. And even with the flashlights they'd given her, lighting was poor. The very idea of doing this with the vision problems the kid had…

"*Hell* no," Sadie muttered at the thought.

How far was she in now? She didn't know. Deep.

Every ten or so steps, she would wave a flashlight along the tunnel walls, hoping to spot the kid's *X*. So far she'd spotted nothing. How deep had the crazy little bugger gone?

Just as she stopped every ten steps or so to shine a flashlight on the tunnel walls in search of a white *X*, so too did Sadie stop every now and then to hold her breath and close her eyes, straining to listen. And just as she had yet to discover any white *X*s, any hint of voices in the distance eluded her all the same.

Sadie carried on undeterred, now adding a third exercise to her journey:

Stop and wave the flashlight on the walls in search of the white *X*.

Stop and listen for voices.

And stop and consider Rafa's offer.

Could she? Could she live out the rest of her existence in their community below ground? Have, as Rafa so succinctly put it, a real life? Before all this nonsense with the Blue, had she not constantly questioned her existence? The aimless wandering, living each day with the very real prospect that it might be her last? And so what if it was? All prospects in the wastelands were transitory anyway. Money. Booze. Sex. All spent as quickly as they arrived. There was no substance up there. No...what was the word she wanted? Structure? No. Well, yes, there was certainly no structure up above, but something else...another word...

Structure.

It *was* structure. Things you could count on. Things you knew would be there for you when you woke in the morning, and the next morning, and the morning after that. With that kind of stability, your prospects could change, become the total antithesis of transitory.

Rafa's words in her head, whether she wanted them or not:

"You will have a chance at an existence where hope is something to be cherished and not feared."

Sadie shook her head.

I gotta kill him. It's the only way.

Rafa's words again:

"Forget this silliness with the Blue gang. Live with us here, where you will be safe."

She snorted to herself.

Safe? A blind kid found this tunnel. How long until one of the Blue discovers it?

An alternate thought pushed its way to the front without conscious effort:

You could always build the wall and never go through. Seal the damn tunnel off and then do as Rafa suggested—live here with them.

Again she shook her head, eyes closed, lips tight.

No. I need to kill him first. Then we seal the tunnel. It's the only way to be sure.

She pushed on. Ten steps. Stop. Wave beams of light over the tunnel walls—

"...a chance at an existence where hope is something to be cherished..."

Would you just shut the hell—

Two things stopped Sadie cold. And it was as though one of those two things had somehow triggered the other, as though the beam of light now illuminating the white *X* on the tunnel wall had triggered the voices in the distance.

twenty-six

The white X on the wall. Voices in the distance. The kid had been dead right…again.

But now are you dead right? Does this tunnel ultimately lie smack beneath the Blue compound? Are those their voices in the distance?

There were two ways for Sadie to find out. Stop here and do her thing in hopes of confirming her suspicions, or venture deeper into the tunnel, closer to the voices. The clarity of her vision would be stronger the closer she got.

Also riskier.

(Confirming if it is actually the Blue compound with only a general layout is useless. I need to find the warlord's chambers.)

You might be able to do that from here.

(And I might not. I can't risk getting too sick if I have to do it twice: once here and, if it proves no good, once more when I'm forced to venture further. I told them I would return healthy enough to fulfill our deal. I need to get closer.)

Sadie's exploratory ritual continued, minus the act of shining one of the flashlights on the tunnel walls in hopes of locating the now-discovered white X. She now kept the flashlight pointed straight ahead, illuminating the darkness for only half a dozen feet or so before it faded to gloom and then black.

And what lies in that black ahead? Stop now and find out.

She pressed on, the remains of her exploratory ritual intact: stop every ten feet or so, close your eyes, hold your breath—

Consider Rafa's offer...

(Shut up. We're not going through this again. Even if I did take Rafa up on his offer and decided to live in their community, don't you think we should know if a murderous gang was living above us???)

*Wall off the tunnel and who would ever know? How long has this community lived—*thrived—*here undisturbed with the tunnel as is? Wall it off and you've all but ensured their existence will flourish forever.*

*(Ensured? Forever? You're starting to think naïvely, just like a mole. Nothing is ever sure. Nothing is forever. Maybe they thrived for as long as they have because they never bothered anyone, never had a crazy warlord combing the wastelands for them. I'd be a liability if I joined their community. I'm not gonna build a wall and back off with my fingers crossed, hoping the bad guys never find me—*find us. *No way. I don't gamble; I cheat. Gambling would be waiting and hoping. Cheating would be killing the son of a bitch. Now PLEASE shut the hell up.)*

Ten more feet. Her flashlight began to dull. She tried shaking it back to life but was soon swallowed in darkness. Fear ticked her spine and raised her pulse, but Sadie and fear had been married their whole existence, for better or for worse. At times he could be her ally, especially during battle, the boosts of adrenaline he gave to help her strike harder, run faster. During times such as now, all he did was make her legs weak, her mouth dry, and her pulse bang her eardrums none too lightly, the fickle bastard.

Sadie tucked the dead flashlight into her satchel and withdrew another one. She clicked it on and was back to where she'd been moments ago—light for a few feet, then gloom, then black.

And of course the voices. The voices were just as much a guide as the light. More so perhaps. Just as she'd learned how peripheral vision could be more reliable than direct line of sight while roaming the desert night, so too did she learn how sometimes sound could be more valuable than sight when homing in on something.

Not that she had many options of travel. The voices were either straight ahead, or she was imagining them. And she wasn't imagining them, unless both she *and* the kid were cuckoo.

Ten more feet. The voices louder now. Laughter, yelling. This had to be it. Had to be. Yet still no entry point in sight.

Perhaps there isn't one. Just because the tunnel might run right beneath the Blue compound doesn't necessarily mean there's access *to that compound via the tunnel. Perhaps the tunnel goes on forever, dumps you out into the middle of nowhere?*

Shit. She'd never thought of that. What if the tunnel *did* bypass the compound? For miles even? Her entire plan would go to hell.

No. Her fever dreams might suck, but they were seldom wrong. Her gut less so. Why else would the boy show her this tunnel in her dreams? The blue *X* instead of the white one he'd actually drawn? There simply was no other explanation. At least none that her stubborn mind was willing to consider just now.

Sadie pressed on, the voices growing, seemingly all around her now. She had to be close.

She aimed the flashlight on the tunnel ceiling as she shuffled forward without care of what might lie straight ahead. She would rather trip or stumble—or, hell, encounter someone or some*thing*—than miss the entry point that *had* to be there, dammit.

The voices began to recede in strength. Was she moving past them? Or were the voices themselves moving?

She kept going, both the flashlight's beam and her eyes still fixed on the ceiling. The voices had receded further still, barely audible now.

We're moving past it.

(We're moving past the voices. It doesn't mean there isn't an entry point up ahead. In fact, so much the better if it's unmanned.)

Maybe, maybe not. Stop here and do your thing. You'll know for sure.

(And if it turns out that the tunnel does go on forever with no entry points? I'd be getting sick for nothing. Why waste it when I can see with my own eyes?)

That's just it. Perhaps you can't *see the entry point with your own eyes.*

(What, like a secret hatch or something? Shut the hell up with that—)

And then the flashlight happened upon it, and the words were out of Sadie's mouth without her realizing. "Holy crap, it's a secret hatch."

.   .   .

The flashlight shone right on it, strong and true. Something that appeared to be a square trapdoor in the ceiling, just big enough to allow a grown man to pass through.

Of course it was no secret hatch; time and disuse had simply eroded its appearance to the point that it appeared to be nothing but a faint sketch of a trapdoor. And Sadie was damn sure the kid hadn't drawn *that* with any chalk.

But how to get up there? Sadie saw no ladders attached to the tunnel wall beneath the hatch as she'd expected to find. She inched closer, waved the flashlight over the wall beneath the hatch, and spotted several small holes in the concrete spaced strategically apart, evidence of where a ladder had once been fixed.

"*Of course*," she muttered to herself. She supposed any number of things could have happened to the ladder. The tunnel was *how* old? Its deepest contents might be a secret to the current community, but what of community members past? She doubted past members knew of its leading into a gang compound; such vital information would have been passed down through generations, warning future ones. Besides, such vital information would have likely resulted in what she was currently proposing to Rafa and the crew: the construction of some kind of wall or barrier to block the damn thing off for good.

And then there was the possibility that the gang compound above hadn't always existed. Perhaps the hatch once led to treacherous grounds above best left unexplored by curious little wanderers—

(kiddo)

—hence the prophylactic measure of removing the ladder just in case.

There were half a dozen more reasons Sadie could entertain. Maybe the stupid ladder had simply *fallen* off the wall, either from time and wear, or perhaps just shoddy design. Either way, it didn't change the fact that there was no ladder. So what now?

Sadie stood on her tiptoes, grunting as she stretched her arm as high as it would go, waving the flashlight all over the trapdoor, desperate to spot something. She spotted a ring. A large ring fixed to a latch pressed flat against the trapdoor. To gain access, one needed to unfold the ring on its latch and then give it a pull. Pull with what, though, was the question. Along with a few others, like: What if the ring was rusted solid to that trapdoor and was unable to unfold? And then, of course, the grand prize winner: What if the trapdoor *itself* was rusted shut? Sadie could sit there and do her martyr thing and get the entire layout of the compound right down to the location of the Blue warlord's toilet, but it would all be for naught if she couldn't get the damn hatch open.

Even though she knew she had nothing on her to accomplish her goal of going up and in, Sadie turned away from the hatch all the same and patted herself down. She had her gun, and she had her knives. She then unslung her satchel and riffled through it—

(*right, because that's where you keep your spare ladder*)

—finding nothing but the dead flashlight and several more fully charged ones. She unsheathed a knife from her waist. If she could get close enough, she could use this to pry the edges of the hatch if they were truly rusted shut. Again, if she could get close enough.

She sheathed the knife and shook her head. Pulled her gun now.

(*Yeah, that's it. Shoot it open, genius. Nice and quiet and totally practical.*)

Sadie cursed under her breath and holstered the gun. She slumped back against one of the tunnel walls, sliding all the way down onto her butt. Her only option now was simple: go all the way back, grab a ladder and tools, and then turn right around and journey on back. She would need help in doing so, someone to point the flashlight while she carried the ladder and tools, or vice versa. Dammit, one of them would have to help—the absolute last thing she wanted.

(*And we're still not sure it actually* is *the Blue compound above, are we? Quite the dilemma: Use your gift now and confirm it's the Blue compound, only to realize your entry point is sealed. Or return with a community member, manage to break that seal, and then use your gift to get the layout of the local brothel above your head.*)

She sighed and waved the flashlight back and forth over the hatch on the ceiling, hoping beyond hope that another alternative would present itself within the vacillating beam.

And one did.

And in a million years, Sadie would have never guessed that the unlikely alternative would be someone opening the hatch for her from the other side.

twenty-seven

The hatch rattled, then stopped. Rattled, then stopped. Rattled a final time and then fell open, the metallic door hitting the tunnel wall with a dull clang as it swung free.

Sadie pulled her gun. Aimed it alongside the flashlight at the now-open hatch, ready for anything.

She saw nothing at first. Just a square opening in the tunnel ceiling that revealed nothing but the darkness beyond.

Did it *fall* open?

She waited, gun and flashlight high and pointed squarely at the open hatch. No way was she about to call out, warn the occupant above that a gun was on them. Such fair-warning nonsense was for the type of fool who still believed in duels.

No, Sadie wanted every conceivable advantage. If a gang member dropped from that ceiling, she was all too happy to give him one hell of a surprise.

What Sadie got instead, however, was the frightened face of a pretty young girl peering down into the tunnel from above. The girl squinted into the flashlight's beam, then—when her eyes settled—saw the gun pointed directly at her, let out a frightened little cry, and pulled her head back inside the hatch, offering Sadie nothing but a square of darkness in the ceiling once again.

No way was that a gang member.

Sadie holstered her gun and stepped forward. "Hello?" she called, trying for firm but nonthreatening.

The girl's face slid into view once more, slow and cautious at first, just enough to get a peek, and then all at once when she saw that Sadie was no longer aiming the gun at her.

"It's okay," Sadie said. "Who are you?"

The girl only continued to stare at Sadie wide-eyed.

"What's your name?" Sadie asked.

"Four," the girl responded. Her voice was as soft and uncertain as her expression.

"Your name is Four?" Sadie said.

The girl nodded.

"Like one, two, three, *four*?" Sadie said.

Again the girl nodded.

"Are you alone?" Sadie asked.

More nodding.

"How did you—?" Sadie shook her head. Get her down first, then question her. *She* might think she's alone, but...

"Come on down from there," Sadie said.

The girl poked her head completely through the hatch now, looking left, then right, and then at Sadie. Her quizzical expression was an easy solve.

"There's no ladder," Sadie said. "I'll catch you though."

"I'm pregnant," the girl said.

"It's okay." Sadie withdrew another flashlight from her satchel and clicked it on. She then removed her satchel from her shoulder and set it against the opposite tunnel wall, positioning both flashlights atop the bag at angles that offered the best possible light toward the hatch and her intended task. Satisfied, Sadie returned beneath the hatch and raised her hands toward the girl, gesturing for her to make her way down.

The girl's wary expression grew.

Sadie tried for a bit of levity. "You'll be fine; I'll break your fall if you lose your grip." She offered a reassuring smile that felt anything but. "Come on—" Sadie gestured with her extended arms once again.

The girl looked behind her through the trapdoor she'd emerged.

"You sure you're alone?" Sadie asked.

"Yes," the girl said. "I'd never have made it this far if I wasn't."

Sadie gestured more urgently with her outstretched arms. "Well, come on then."

· · ·

The girl inched her way down feet-first, carefully worming from one side to the other during her descent in order to protect her belly from the unforgiving edges of the hatch. When Sadie was able, she took hold of the girl by the ankles, then the knees, and then finally, gingerly, by the waist to help guide her down. There had been a moment of pause when the girl was afraid to take that final leap and let go of her grip on the ledge above, yet Sadie had presented her options in her typical curt fashion: "You can either let go or pull yourself back up. Which sounds easier to you?"

The girl let go, and Sadie braced for the extra weight, grunting for a brief moment when she took the girl whole in her arms, and then exhaling when she finally lowered her to the tunnel floor.

Sadie guessed the girl at no more than fifteen. She appeared waiflike, big innocent eyes and all. Her hair was long and dirty blonde, slightly unkempt either from her journey below or neglect. Or both. The beige sundress she wore (it too ruffled and marked either from her journey or neglect or both) held the ability to display both a skinny girl and a pregnant one, with its thin shoulder straps showcasing bony shoulders and arms, and then its above-knee height that made the dress billow, amplifying the fullness of her belly. On the girl's feet were tattered slippers. This time neglect and not the journey was the obvious culprit for their state; Sadie had spotted the worn soles with holes on the balls of the feet when the girl first began to wiggle out of the hatch.

"So, your name's Four?" Sadie asked.

Four nodded.

There would be time to ask what, when, where, and how (even though Sadie already had a pretty good idea—all except for the most important *how*, of course), but right now there were far more urgent matters to attend to as far as Sadie was concerned. Matters like closing the door to the hatch for the time being. The girl claimed she was alone and not followed, but even the dimmest of gang members, if sent to look for the missing girl, would think an open trapdoor in the floor of their compound—one that had likely been secretive up until then—was a pretty solid clue as to the direction she'd ventured.

"Listen, Four," Sadie began, gesturing to the open door above, "we're going to have to shut that door up there. You don't want anyone to know you're here, right?"

Four nodded emphatically, clutching her belly with both hands. "I want to protect my baby."

"We'll get into all that later," Sadie said. "Right now we've got to figure out a way to close that door."

Four nodded again.

To Sadie, there seemed to be only two logical choices—one risky; the other safe, but more than a little cumbersome.

"Here's what we can do," Sadie began. "We can venture all the way back through this tunnel—and it's a ways, trust me—grab a ladder, and then return here and shut the door to the hatch that way. Or..." She sighed. "You can get on my shoulders, and we can shut it right now."

"Get on your shoulders?" Four said, as though she too wasn't wild about the idea.

"I could always get on yours..." Sadie waved a hand up and down the girl's scrawny frame. "Except you don't strike me as the physical type. Plus you're shorter than me. *Plus* you're pregnant—" Sadie stopped, frowned, and shook her head. "Let's just get it over with."

twenty-eight

Rafa, Izar, and Teir waited patiently by the tunnel entrance for Sadie's return. They dispersed periodically, but only in shifts. Twice for bathroom breaks, and once for Rafa to bring water and snacks to tide them over during their wait. Teir was delighted to see that some of those snacks consisted of Fahima's cricket and sowbug cookies, offering ever so politely to take the bunch off Rafa and Izar's hands if they didn't want them.

Rafa, handing the cookies over to Teir with a smile, said: "Who do you think I brought them for?"

Teir shoved one of the cookies into his mouth whole and mumbled a crumb-filled thanks.

Izar, nibbling on a cricket bar, turned to Rafa. "Feels like she's been in there forever."

Rafa nodded and sipped water from one of the canteens Izar had brought. He'd chosen not to eat; anxiety had snuffed his appetite.

"Told you it went on forever," Teir said after chasing his mouthful of cookie with water from his canteen.

"I truly hope that's the only reason it's been so long," Rafa said.

"She'll be sick when she returns," Izar said to Rafa.

"Yes. Though she claims the sickness won't be as bad as before."

"Are we prepared just in case?"

"Yes."

"What if—"

"*Look*," Rafa blurted, pointing into the tunnel.

The faint glow of not one, but two flashlights bobbed in the distant black of the tunnel.

"Why is she using *two* rowlights?" Rafa said.

Izar pulled the Beretta. "Maybe she's not alone."

"She would never lead anyone back here," Teir said. "She'd sooner die."

Izar popped the clip on the Beretta, checked the rounds, and then slammed the clip back home. She gave both Rafa and Teir a quick glance. "Get behind me," she told them.

The dual flashlights continued forward. Izar raised the gun and took aim.

The flashlights soon stopped their approach. A voice echoed from within the tunnel: "*Whoa! Don't shoot!*"

"*Sadie?*" Izar called.

"Yeah, it's me," Sadie called back.

Izar lowered the gun and squinted into the tunnel. She could just make out the silhouettes of two figures approaching. "Are you okay?" she asked.

"Fine—we'll be there in a minute."

Izar and Rafa exchanged a look. Rafa said: "Who's 'we'?"

.   .   .

After a short visit in the infirmary with Elixa, they were back in Rafa and Teir's apartment, the newest addition a fifteen-year-old pregnant girl (just shy of five months along, and while a bit undernourished, in decent health, according to Elixa) who'd recently escaped the Blue compound via the very method Sadie had, and still, intended to enter.

So many questions.

"So you feared that if your child was a girl, the warlord would murder it?" Izar asked.

Four nodded. "The General only wants males to carry on his legacy."

Sadie snorted. "*Legacy.*"

Four continued. "I knew once I gave birth, The General would have me banished to the outskirts of the wastelands to die; he has no taste for us after we give birth. I'd grown to accept the fact that my time left was short. But I could not accept the possibility of my child joining me in the wastelands if it were to be a girl."

"You're very brave," Izar said.

"Why does he call you Four?" Teir piped up.

Four gave a helpless little shrug. "None of us that serve The General have names, only numbers."

Sadie broke in. "Okay, so now we *have* to kill him. We've got no choice."

"Why do you say that?" Rafa asked.

"Because now they're not just gonna be looking for me, they're gonna be looking for her too—" She gestured toward Four. "How soon do you think it'll be before they find out how she managed to escape? Find out about the hatch?"

"How certain are you the hatch remains secretive among the Blue gang?" Rafa asked Four.

"Fairly certain, I guess. I'd never heard The General or any of his men mention it before, only us."

"*Us?*" Izar said. "Why would the slaves know about it and not the general or his men?"

"It was a myth," Four said. "We spoke of it in hope, but never truly believed it existed. To entertain its existence was our only true escape."

"But it *wasn't* a myth," Rafa said.

"No."

"And what made you take such a leap of faith?" Izar asked. "How would you even know where to begin?"

Tears welled up in Four's eyes. "Seven," she said softly.

"Another slave?" Izar asked.

Four nodded. "She'd already given birth. It was a boy, so the child was safe, but Seven knew her time was limited. She used that time to look. It was not easy; we're always watched. She went days without sleep in her quest."

"Where would she even begin to look?" Izar asked again.

"As the myth of the tunnel grew among us, so did our reasoning as to where it must lie. We had several theories; Seven explored them all."

"And found the winner," Izar said.

Four nodded.

"Wait—I saw that hatch," Sadie began. "That door looked as if it hadn't been opened in decades, if ever. The ladder on the wall beneath it was even gone. No way your friend Seven went through that hatch before you to confirm anything."

"I never said she did," Four said. "Just that she'd located it…or what she'd hoped was it."

"Why didn't she go with you?" Rafa asked.

"That was our plan." Four began tearing up again. "Well, at least that was *my* plan. Seven had a different one in mind."

"Like what?" Rafa said.

"Causing a distraction. She kissed me goodbye and insisted I go alone. Before I could object, she fled to a far corner of the compound, far away from the hatch's whereabouts, and started a great fire. When gang members tended to the fire, she attacked them. Even The General got involved, the commotion was so great." Tears began rolling down both cheeks. "She gave her life for me and my child."

"My word," Izar said. "You still took one heck of a risk. Your friend had never been through the hatch. Sadie claims it was exceptionally weathered. Suppose you couldn't get it open?"

"She did, though," Sadie said. "And here we are." She turned to Rafa. "I'll admit; I considered your offer on my way down that tunnel. Thought about leaving the Blue warlord alone and building that wall. I'm still all for building the wall, but as far as leaving the warlord be—no freaking way."

"Why?" Rafa asked.

"Like I said a few minutes ago, they're not just looking for me now, they're looking for her, and more importantly, her child. *The Blue warlord's child.* Me? Your suggestion about walling up that tunnel and hiding out down here might have worked. The world's a big place and I had one hell of a head start. It's possible they'd have eventually given up looking for me. Her?" She pointed to Four. "Her starting point was the compound. They're gonna be thinking she snuck on past them when they were distracted by the commotion her friend caused, or she found another way. Guarantee you they're combing a decent radius on the outskirts of the compound right now, looking for her. When they don't find her, it won't be long until they start to suspect some other means of escape. Something *literally* right under their feet the entire time."

"But if we build the wall…" Rafa said.

"You don't think they'll break it down?"

Izar frowned. "Well, then why did you suggest building it at all?"

"Because no one knew about the hatch but us," Sadie replied. "If the Blue *did* happen to find the hatch one day, the wall would be just a deterrent in a dark tunnel hundreds of yards long; no need to question the wall's existence, just a round of shrugs and back up the way they came with no story to tell. But now? Once they figure out Four didn't miraculously slip past them and isn't wandering aimlessly, half-dead in the wastelands? That wall won't be a deterrent; it'll be one hell of a clue as to which way she went, *especially* when they see that it's freshly built."

"So, forget the wall entirely, is that it?" Izar asked.

"Of course not," Sadie said. "My logic about the wall's potential as a deterrent stands. But that logic relies on time, you follow me?"

"If someone finds the wall years from now, there's very little reason to question it. Especially if it's years old," Rafa said. "If someone finds the wall now, looking freshly built, it serves as a clue that someone is trying to keep something out."

"*Exactly,*" Sadie said. "The only way we're going to keep them from nosing around and finding the hatch is to kill the warlord and watch their priorities crumble."

"But you were unable to use your gift to get the layout of the compound," Rafa said. "To obtain the precise whereabouts of the warlord's quarters."

"Then I'll have to go back into the tunnel."

"*I* can tell you about The General's quarters," Four said.

"I'd rather see it with my own eyes," Sadie replied.

"Why not hear what she has to say first?" Izar said.

"No."

"Why?" Rafa asked. "Would you agree that Four's escape from the Blue gang's compound through the hatch has caused greater urgency in our plans?"

"Of course."

"Well, then we need to adjust those plans. The constraints of time have forced it upon us."

"*Change the plan?*"

"No—adjust it," Rafa said. "Expedite it. I won't try to change your mind about killing the Blue gang's warlord; I know how resolute you are in your belief that it is the right thing to do. However, we no longer have time on our side. Your venture into the tunnel was long. If you were to do it again, utilize your gift, then return to me to be healed of your sickness, only to go *back* to the tunnel to fulfill your mission..." Rafa splayed his hands. "Can you not see how time-consuming it would all be? You said it yourself—before, when the Blue gang thought you could be anywhere, there was no urgency to find you; you *did* have time. Now, with the addition of Four, time is what we *don't* have."

"That's true," Four said. "There *was* no urgency to find you. The General gave the order to wait on the hunt for the martyr. It's how two of his men ended up missing."

All heads swung towards Four.

It was Sadie who said: "Huh?"

"The General wants to find you, that's true," Four began, "but he gave the order to wait. Two of his men didn't listen, though—they went looking for you themselves."

"How do you know this?" Izar asked.

"I heard it. I hear a lot."

"Wait, so these two men went missing?" Sadie asked.

Four nodded.

"And what? Your general thinks I killed *them* too?"

"No—he thinks someone named Finn did. No, wait...he thinks Finn *brought* them to someone. Someone named Vidar."

Sadie whistled and took a step back, eyes unavoidably wider.

"What?" Rafa asked. "You know this Finn? This Vidar?"

"I know Finn. Vidar I know *of*. They might be the only two people on this planet that want the Blue deader than I do."

"Who are they?" Rafa asked.

"Finn's a bounty hunter. Vidar's an arms dealer. The Blue warlord murdered Vidar's family. They've been at war ever since. Finn's not particularly fond of the Blue either. Vidar's son was Finn's friend."

Izar leaned in, eager. "Perhaps we should go to them for assistance!"

Sadie raised a hand. "Whoa—what's this 'we' stuff? I told you, you guys weren't involved. This is all me."

"The plans have changed, though," Izar said. She then gestured to Four. "As Rafa says, the addition of the girl has changed them."

"Yeah, I heard what he said. And he's right; time is a luxury we don't have anymore. But no way are you guys getting involved. Plus, I'm not about to start poking my nose around that compound unless I've seen every inch of it with *my own eyes.*"

Rafa turned to Four. "How well do you know the compound?"

"Fairly well. Most of my time was spent in The General's quarters, though."

Sadie splayed a hand. "There, you see? She might know his quarters inside and out, but how to *get* to those quarters? I can't afford to be going left when I need to be going right. The tiniest little mistake could be my life."

"I know the way," Four said earnestly. "How do you suppose *I* was able to escape on my first attempt?"

"You said your friend caused a distraction," Sadie said. "One hell of a fire. And then proceeded to attack anyone that intervened."

"True—but I was still a pregnant slave making her way down to a mysterious exit I had yet to see for myself. I was able to find it because Seven and I had gone over its location countless times. If someone like me was able to make her way based only on the words of another, surely someone as capable as you could do the same."

Everyone looked at Sadie. Sadie rolled her eyes. "Challenging my ego now, are we?" She looked at Four. "You sure you're only fifteen? You've the psychology thing down pretty damn good."

"I was taken from my family when I was eleven. My mother and father believed strongly in education."

"Where are they now?" Izar asked.

"Dead."

A moment of uncomfortable silence.

"Dead by the Blue warlord's hand, I assume?" Izar then asked.

Four nodded.

Izar turned to Sadie. "This Finn and Vidar, they too are victims of the Blue warlord's cruelty. I still propose we, sorry, *you* go to them for assistance in your attack. They would surely jump at the opportunity, yes?"

"What *opportunity*?" Sadie said. "Nothing's changed. If it was so easy to destroy the Blue compound, you don't think Vidar would have done it ages ago? Just because little ole me now wants them dead too doesn't change a thing."

"Vidar and his men can enter from the hatch just as you plan to!" Izar said.

Sadie laughed. "Right. 'File on up one at a time, fellas! And, Blue gang, do you mind waiting until all of us are up before you start attacking?'"

Teir chuckled at Sadie's sarcasm. Izar frowned at Teir, then turned back to Sadie. "Don't mock me," she said. "I mention the hatch as simply another means of attack. Much like Four's friend created the fire as a diversion, so too could a proper army create a diversion from above while soldiers infiltrate from below."

That's actually not a bad idea, Sadie thought with some reluctance. *Infantry attacks the perimeter from above and keeps them busy while the big dogs sneak in from below and take out the heart. But still...*

"Look, it's not a bad idea," she began, "but even if I wanted to go along with it, I wouldn't even know where to begin to find Finn, much less Vidar."

"Then at least allow Four to give you the layout of the compound," Rafa said. "The two of you may use me and Teir's apartment. Teir and I can stay with Fahima."

Teir said: "Huh?"

"Think of the cookies," Izar said to him.

Sadie shook her head. "I don't like this."

"Think of the time it will save," Rafa said. "If Four's information is sound, and you become confident in your recall, you could venture up far sooner. In the meantime, we will gather supplies and helpers to wall up the tunnel."

"What about your Clear?" Sadie said.

"Do you feel able to go this evening?" Rafa asked.

"Sure," Sadie said. "On one condition."

"Are you renegotiating?" Izar asked.

"No—but the plans have changed, remember?" she said a little condescendingly. "I'm simply adjusting them to better suit my needs."

Rafa and Izar exchanged another look. Rafa said: "What is your one condition?"

"If I go tonight and find you your Clear, and then return sick, you would fix me up, right?"

Rafa nodded.

"Well, then if I'm gonna get sick, I'm gonna make the most of it." She kept her eyes on Rafa and Izar, yet pointed at Four. "When I get back with your Clear, I'm getting in her head—see what she knows with *my own eyes*. None of this *telling me* shit. Once I'm satisfied, you can fix me up just as you'd have done anyway. Two birds, one stone. We got a deal?"

Izar gestured to Four. "I think she's the one you need to be asking."

Sadie turned to Four. "What do you say?"

"Get in my head? You mean read my mind?" Four asked.

Sadie nodded. "It won't hurt."

"Speak for yourself," Teir muttered.

twenty-nine

General Gash had learned long ago that anger clouded judgment. Led to impulsive responses as opposed to strategic ones.

His wenches were lined up on their knees before him, five of them now instead of seven—the very reason for this assembly. Both shackled young men were on their knees and before their master as well. Despite his disciplined calm, it was still apparent General Gash was suppressing a frightening rage. Even his own men kept a safe distance within his quarters. Only Wrath dared stand close.

Gash walked up and down the line of young men and women on their knees. An axe dangled from his right hand, periodically bumping against his thigh as he considered his row of insignificants.

"Wrath," he said, calmly addressing his number one without taking his good eye off the line before him. "How many do you count here?"

"Seven," Wrath replied.

Gash nodded. "I too count seven. I count seven *in total*. How many wenches do you count, Wrath?"

"Five," Wrath replied.

"Five, yes…" Gash paused before one of the young women. Gently touched the blade of the axe against the center part of her long blonde hair and held it there. The girl began to whimper. "That means two are missing, am I right?"

"One is missing. The other is very dead," Wrath said with his tooth-less grin.

"Are you sure?" Gash said.

Wrath produced the severed head of Seven and held it by the scalp for all the line to see. They all whimpered now, the boys too.

"Yes," Gash said, "she does appear to be very dead." He inched down the line, stopping at the next girl, gently tracing the blade of the axe along the soft flesh of this one's cheek. "Which number is that you're holding?" he asked Wrath.

"Seven," Wrath replied.

Gash now tapped the blade of the axe against the girl's cheek. "Which number are you?" he asked her.

"Two," she managed.

Gash then addressed the remaining four girls, asking them to verify their numbers, the blade of the axe caressing each as he did so. Their replies were weak and frightened, but swift.

"One, Two, Three, Five, Six…" Gash said. He set the axe aside and strolled toward Wrath, took Seven's severed head from him and then returned to the line, blindly rolling the head from one hand to the other as though absently fiddling with a ball. "We now know the fate that befell Seven, yes?" he asked the group, the act of brandishing Seven's head to underline his query highly unnecessary for the horrified row. "So I believe that just leaves Four?"

No reply.

Gash tossed the head to Wrath with all the casual interest of two guys playing catch. He picked up the axe again. "Am I to assume then, by your silence, that you disagree with me? Four is *not* missing?"

The line fervently shook their heads. There was hope and mercy pleading from their eyes, the will to live snuffing reason; they knew few would survive the next few minutes, if any.

"Okay then," Gash said, "Four *is* missing. Far more importantly, my *unborn child* is missing. Who would now like to tell me where Four went?"

The line exchanged frantic looks, seemingly desperate one or the other might provide an answer though it was blatantly apparent they had none.

Gash addressed Wrath again without taking his eye off the line. "Wrath, are you aware of the ancient practice of slaughtering a chicken to scare a monkey?"

"Can't say I am," Wrath replied.

"The concept is very simple. Nomads often trained monkeys and used them to entertain patrons. Sometimes the monkeys would tire and refuse to perform. The nomads would then promptly produce a chicken and slaughter it before the monkey's eyes, sending a message to the monkey that he should continue to perform lest he suffer the same fate. It never failed. What I have before me now, Wrath, is a row of monkeys. I need a chicken to slaughter for the rest to see."

Wrath grinned. The line whimpered louder. Gash raised the axe over his shoulder and strolled the line. Stopped, spun, and lunged at one of his guards who stood nearby, burying the axe deep into his head. The man dropped hard and dead. Gash released the handle, and the axe remained stuck in the man's skull, the handle standing erect as the man's body twitched.

Everyone gasped. Even Wrath.

Gash turned and splayed his hands before the line. "There—I've slaughtered my chicken. Are my monkeys ready to perform now?"

.   .   .

After an hour of interrogation, and one more of his men playing hapless chicken to his row of monkeys, General Gash had gotten nowhere. Though his rage was increasing by the minute, he was not allowing it to cloud all reason; he could tell his monkeys did indeed know nothing.

The remainder of his men now (gratefully) ushered out, and alone in his quarters with only Wrath, the line of shackled young men and wenches—still kneeling, not daring to move—and the bodies of the two men who'd unwittingly played their part as chickens, Gash retook his throne.

"Gin," he called to the kneeling shackled boys. "And do I even need to remind you what happened to the last one of you idiots who spilled my drink?"

Both boys shook their heads. They then exchanged looks, apparently unsure which was to go fetch their master his gin.

"Let's go!" Gash yelled.

They both stood, both scurrying to the bar in the far corner of their master's quarters to prepare his drink.

"Tell me something, General," Wrath began, gesturing towards the two dead gang members on the floor. "Why this?" He then gestured toward the kneeling girls and then toward the boys in the far corner of the quarters preparing Gash his gin. "I would have thought one of *them* would have sufficed in being your chickens."

"And your thinking is why you're not fit to be general."

Wrath frowned.

Gash smiled and waved a placating hand at his number one. "I meant no insult. You're brave and loyal—a trait as rare as Clear—but you are a soldier, not a leader. Had I chosen to take the life of any one of *them*"—now it was Gash who gestured towards the kneeling girls and then the boys preparing the drink—"I might have been killing the very one who *did* know something. By killing one of my rabble—and they *are* mere rabble, Wrath; meat puppets, all of them—I was sending a much harsher message while preserving the tongues of those who might be able to tell me something useful. Do you agree?"

Wrath offered up a slow nod. "It shocked even me; I confess."

Gash smiled again. "And this from a man who wears teeth around his neck."

Wrath grinned, the gap where his front teeth once were ever noticeable.

"Besides," Gash continued, motioning to the two dead gang members sprawled out on the floor, "I didn't particularly care for those two. Meat puppets they all might be, but I found their particular grade of meat to be poor. Perhaps after a bit of butchering, we can pawn them off as camel meat to local nomads, see if my assessment of their quality is accurate."

Wrath broke out into laughter.

Both boys now approached with the general's drink. They carried it with the care of a pressure-sensitive explosive. It arrived without a drop spilled.

He took his drink and drank deeply. He then patted his broad shoulders. "One of you up here." He bent forward and patted his thick calves. "One of you down here."

The boys hurried to their positions and went to work massaging their master.

"What have we gotten from any of this, though, General?" Wrath said. "You seem confident your wenches and bitch boys know nothing. Have you considered any of your men?"

"I have. They have nothing to gain from keeping anything from me. Quite the contrary; they would have much to gain should they divulge anything useful. Much like the two idiots who went looking for the martyr even after I gave the order to wait, the opportunity to curry my favor would be a foolish thing to pocket."

"Speaking of the martyr…" Wrath said.

Gash sipped his gin and placed his good eye on Wrath. "Yes?"

"Still think there's a connection between her, Finn, and Vidar?"

"If there is, I believe the connection is coincidental. However, all three do share *us* as a common enemy. Such a thing is something we shouldn't lose sight of."

Wrath frowned. "What about Four? Think they had anything to do with Four's escape?"

Gash placed his eye on Wrath again. "And what motive could they possibly have for doing that? Never mind the means."

Wrath shrugged. "No idea. I'm just saying a lot of crazy shit has happened in the past few weeks, and it all seemed to start with that martyr bitch killing one of ours. You know how spooky those freaks can be. I can't give you a motive, but she'd be a good choice for helping to pull off a disappearing act like Four did."

Gash digested his number one's assessment. Wrath's reasoning held improbable probability. Its ambiguity burned Gash's practiced calm until his stoic manner suddenly broke. He tossed his cup of gin across the room and kicked the boy at his feet in the face. The boy rolled onto his side in a fetal ball, clutching his face and whimpering.

Wrath smirked down at the writhing boy. Then: "We're gonna find your baby and the disobedient whore who carries it, General. At her age, in her condition, there's only so many places she can hide."

"And if your notion is correct? The martyr *is* somehow involved? Finn and Vidar?"

Wrath fingered the sizeable scar on his neck. "Then we go to war."

Gash, regaining his calm as quickly as he'd lost it, unsheathed a large knife from his waist and began whittling into the armrest of his throne, his response taking on an entranced quality, as though unaware he was thinking aloud. "Yes…such an eventuality was inevitable, wasn't it?"

Wrath gestured to the two dead men on the floor. "Just don't kill any more. We'll need the puppets."

Quip or truth, and it was both, Gash did not acknowledge his number one's comment. He just continued whittling, dreaming, envisioning the carnage he'd always known would one day come.

thirty

Teir had easily agreed to remain behind with Four while Rafa and Izar accompanied Sadie to locate Clear. Despite her miraculously good health, the girl was nonetheless in a state of shock, yet she seemed comfortable with Teir. And though still melancholy and subdued as a result of his recent ordeal, Teir had accepted the responsibility of looking after their guest with a grace and maturity that had made Rafa immeasurably proud.

Now, as Rafa followed his sister and Sadie deeper into the cave, scraping his shins, knees, and elbows as he climbed over jagged rocks, his relief that the two adolescents were safe at home increased exponentially. He almost wished he were home with them, but his intense scientific curiosity overrode his discomfort, as it so often did.

"Almost there," Sadie called back to him and Izar.

"How are you feeling?" Rafa asked her.

"Like it's the morning after a long night of bad gin."

Rafa and Izar both remained quiet.

"I don't suppose you two can relate," Sadie added.

"There's a tribe we trade with from whom I've purchased very fine whiskey, which I quite enjoy," Izar told her. "But I've never indulged to the point of illness."

"A mole with a taste for fine guns *and* fine booze," Sadie said. "You're really screwing with my preconceived notions, you know."

"As are you with mine," Izar countered.

"Really? How so?"

"I imagined that a…person of your kind, who had managed to survive more than three decades of life, would by now be severely compromised by your gift, physically and psychologically. Yet I see no evidence of that in you at all."

Sadie chuckled bitterly. "You may change your mind once you get to know me better."

"I don't think I will change my mind, but I do hope to get to know you better."

Sadie laughed quietly without bitterness this time. "Jeez. *Both* of you now with the hard sell on me sticking around."

"You have little to lose and much to gain from staying with us," Izar said matter-of-factly, her tone at once authoritative and maternal. She sounded so much like their mother that Rafa felt a chill move through him that had nothing to do with the cool air in the cave.

.   .   .

They traveled in silence for a while, picking their way carefully, the cave narrowing and becoming increasingly inhospitable as they moved deeper.

Rafa had just misjudged his ability to scale a particularly large and jagged rock, resulting in a painful fall that almost certainly left him with a sprained ankle and scrambling to catch up with the two women.

When he finally joined them, they stood at the entrance of a small chamber, staring at the pale, granular substance covering the walls and floor. It shimmered beneath the beam of Sadie's rowlight.

"That's it?" Izar asked, her tone conveying mild disappointment.

"Yeah," Sadie replied weakly, the cost of her chore now in full effect. The beam from her rowlight wavered as she wiped her sweaty brow with the other hand. "What did you expect?"

"I don't know," Izar said. "But that just looks like glittery white sand to me."

"Well, it's not," Sadie assured her.

"How is it administered?" Rafa asked.

"However you can stand to get it into you."

"Can you ingest it?"

"If you want. It tastes about a million times worse than the worst thing you ever tasted though." She wiped her brow again, her color becoming not unlike the Clear before them. "Now fill your containers with the stuff so we can get the hell out of here before you have to carry me home again."

Rafa wasted no time doing as he was told.

. . .

The three returned to the community several hours later. Rafa was scraped, bruised, sprained, and exhausted, but in no way did this diminish his elation at their accomplishment. Elation that was shared—and exponentially increased—by the small crowd that greeted them.

Julen stood at the front of the crowd and gave his son a curt nod before corralling Izar to obtain a briefing.

She grabbed Rafa's arm as their father began to lead her away.

"Take care of Sadie," she told him. "I'll catch up with you later." She flashed Rafa a warm smile and added: "*Lo hiciste bien, hermanito.*" Then she departed.

Elixa emerged in their wake, outstretched arms embracing her grandson tightly.

"My darling boy, I'm so proud of you."

His quickly murmured "thank you" was out of obligation and nothing more. Though he knew her words were sincere, he felt that her gratitude was misplaced: Teir had found Sadie, and Sadie had found them a rather large pocket of Clear...and was now suffering the consequences.

Rafa had a patient to attend to.

As if she could read her grandson's single-minded thoughts, Elixa shooed the crowd back with firm words and gestures, which were instantly obeyed, and led the way to the infirmary.

. . .

As soon as the worst of Sadie's symptoms had been alleviated, she insisted they return to his apartment.

"You need rest," Rafa told her. Although he wanted to check in on Teir and the girl, he was extremely eager to examine the Clear they had obtained, to begin learning about this elusive substance that was as mysterious as it was powerful.

"I'll rest when I'm laid to rest," Sadie replied as she pulled on her boots and rose from the bed. "Right now I need to get in that kid's head and plan my next move."

Rafa shook his head and uttered a sigh of resignation.

· · ·

Rafa opened the door to the apartment and was greeted by the sound of youthful laughter and a pleasant sight: Teir and Four sat across from each other at the dining table playing cards.

"You *have* to be cheating," she complained through her giggles.

Teir's outrage was clearly tempered by amusement. "I am *not* cheating!"

"You're *blind*, and you just beat me for the third time in a row!"

"You don't need perfect vision to be a master strategist," he informed her, echoing Rafa's own words that he'd spoken to Teir on numerous occasions.

The girl turned to Rafa and Sadie as they entered the apartment. "You're back."

"Rafa?" Teir rose from the table and crossed the room quickly. "Did you find Clear?"

"Of course we did," Sadie answered as she walked past Teir to stand over the girl still seated at the table. "And now the party's over. C'mon, Four—I need a look inside your head."

"Her name isn't *Four*," Teir said sharply. "It's Dakota."

Rafa and Sadie exchanged glances, then both turned to the girl.

"You can call me Koty," she told them.

Sadie nodded. "All right, Koty. Let's sit on the couch. This isn't nearly as much fun as losing at cards to a good-looking guy, so we might as well be comfortable."

thirty-one

Sadie seldom had an audience for what she was about to do. At least not a cognizant one.

"Ready?" she asked Koty. Sadie sat comfortably next to the girl on the couch, yet to place a hand on her. Rafa, Izar, and Teir stood watching from a distance fueled more by awe than fear.

"You sure it won't hurt?" Koty asked.

"Only about one in five die when I do it."

Koty's eyes bugged out of her head.

"I'm kidding. Give me your hands."

Koty hesitated.

"Listen," Sadie began, "I'd be lying if I said there won't be the possibility of residual effects afterwards. But they aren't physically painful." She shot a brief and somewhat guilty eye toward Teir.

"Residual effects?" Koty said.

Sadie sighed. "Yeah, it's kinda tough to explain, because even *I* don't really understand it. Let's just say that after it's over, you and I will have a stronger connection up here." She tapped her finger against her temple.

"I'll become a martyr too?"

"No, no…" She sighed again. "See, it's hard to —" Sadie stopped mid-sentence and turned towards Teir. "Take the kid over there. Ever since

I got into his head, he and I have had…I don't know, a connection. Except the connection's run by a shoddy wire. It works when it works, you know?"

Koty still looked anxious.

Sadie tried for a bit of levity.

"How about this? When we're done, there's a chance I might be able to tell Teir if you think he's cute or not," she said.

"*Huh?*" Teir blurted.

Koty blushed and fought a smile.

"You ready now?" Sadie asked.

Koty nodded.

"Give me your hands."

Koty placed her hands into Sadie's.

Sadie closed her eyes. Took a deep breath, exhaling long and slow.

Rafa, Izar, and Teir looked on, their interest immovable.

Sadie entered Koty's mind…

…and then promptly exited.

"I've seen enough," she said, taking her hands off Koty and hopping to her feet.

"*What?*" Izar asked. "You did it for all of ten seconds. Is that as long as it takes?"

"No," Teir answered softly.

Rafa glanced at Teir before turning his attention back to Sadie. "Is something wrong?"

Sadie gave a pained chuckle. "The place is a damned fortress."

"So what does that mean?" Izar asked.

Sadie paused for a moment, sighed, and eventually said: "It means you might have been on to something when you suggested an army could preoccupy them with an attack from above while a second army goes through the tunnel and hits them from below." She shook her head. "Dammit."

Everyone silently digested Sadie's implication.

"Would it be so hard to find this Finn you mentioned?" Izar eventually asked.

Sadie sighed again. "I could find him if I had to. I was just hoping I wouldn't have to."

"You two don't get along?" Rafa asked.

"We used to."

Izar gave an understanding little smile. "Heartbreak, was it?"

"You'll have to ask him," Sadie said. "I didn't hang around long enough to find out."

thirty-two

"Good whiskey," Finn said to the bartender.

"You got it, Finn." The bartender, the same rail-thin bespectacled man sporting a brown derby atop a head of greasy black hair that had served Finn not long ago, ducked behind the bar and produced a bottle.

Finn took a stool and poured himself a shot, immediately pouring himself a second before he'd finished swallowing the first.

"You know last time you were in here?" the bartender began. "With them two members of the Blue?"

"Yeah?"

The bartender leaned in, his breath like spoiled meat. Finn frowned and leaned back, waving the man's breath away as though it were smoke. The bartender took notice and pursed his lips, leaning back to his station a respectable distance behind the bar. "Trench mouth," he said through tight lips. "Nothing I can do about it."

"Ever thought about brushing your teeth?"

"I think I'm well past that stage. Only option it would appear I have now is to find a dentist; and no way am I about to let one of them butchers come near me. There was this guy once in Partlow? Apparently he—"

"I don't give a shit about your stupid teeth." Finn ran a hand back and forth over his shaved head in frustration, then poured himself another shot. "Finish saying what you were saying—about the two members of the Blue I was drinking with last time."

The bartender nodded quickly, his face an earnest apology for forgetting his place. "Right…well, word is they're both gone."

Finn's expression never once flickered; he maintained a face of only mild interest throughout. "Gone where?"

"*Gone*…as in missing," the bartender said.

Finn splayed a hand. "And this has anything to do with me how?"

The bartender frowned and pushed his spectacles further up his nose, his confused expression giving the clear read that the implication was obvious. "Well, you were the last to be seen with them, weren't you?" he asked.

"How the hell should I know? When I left those two drinking, they were well on their way to being brain dead, more so. Chances are they got themselves into a mess of trouble after they left." Finn suddenly frowned, annoyed. He had intentionally left early while drinking with the two members of the Blue so patrons and bartenders would take notice, give him an alibi. "You telling me you didn't see me leave while they were still here?" He pointed to a table behind him. "There, at that table? It wasn't that long ago."

Whether he truly did remember or was just plain scared of Finn's growing irritation, the bartender appeared sincere when he stuttered out: "No, I remember you leaving…I remember, I remember."

"So then why are you saying I was the last to be seen with them? Hell, technically *you* were the last to be seen with them, you gossipy little prick." Finn kicked back his stool and stood. Leaned over the bar and grabbed the bartender by the shirt and pulled him close. "Turn your face away from me so I don't have to smell that outhouse you call a mouth." The bartender did, giving Finn his ear. "Whatever happened to those two gang members has nothing to do with me. But when you start running your rotted little mouth, giving people ideas that I'm somehow responsible for their disappearance—"

"I never said you was—"

Finn shook him once, hard. "Shut up. You're a damn bartender; all you people do is talk shit. Now, it's no secret around here that I don't get along with the Blue, but they've let me be for a long time. You start spouting off about me killing two of their—"

"I never said—"

Finn now gripped his throat, cutting his words off at the source. "Nothing ever needs to be said outright to make some bullshit flourish. You should know that better than anyone, bartender."

Finn then lowered his head, exhaled long and slow. He did not like losing his cool in public. But the effort he'd gone through to establish an alibi for the disappearance of the two Blue members, only for the truth to surface and inevitably find the ear of the Blue warlord thanks to some gossipy trench-mouthed bartender…he should do the son of a bitch a favor and knock every one of his rotted teeth out of his head right now.

Finn raised his head. The word had assuredly already spread, the damage done, but Finn said it all the same: "So…tell me again who the last person to be seen with those two Blue members was."

"I truly don't know," the bartender garbled out, Finn's hand still on his throat.

Finn nodded. "Good. If someone pulls up a stool here and says they heard *Finn* was the last to be seen with them, what might you say to that, you think?"

"I'd say they was dead wrong."

Finn cracked a humorless little smile at the man's choice of words. "Dead right." He shoved the bartender back, snatched up his bottle and glass, and headed for a table.

.   .   .

"*Asshole*," Finn muttered to himself before downing another shot.

Yes, he hated the Blue. And yes, he had gladly delivered those two idiots over to Vidar. Would gladly hand *all* members of the Blue over to Vidar. But he wasn't foolish enough to start a war.

At least not outright.

There *was* a war going on as far as Finn was concerned; he would always want every one of the Blue dead for what they'd done to Vidar's family, his friend Sten especially. But to declare an open war would be foolhardy. Even Vidar wasn't brash enough to do such a thing. The Blue compound was heavily guarded, heavily fortified, Gash's quarters somewhere deep within.

Vidar had always talked of one day waging an outright war. Of exacting *true* revenge, wiping the Blue out completely, taking Gash's scalp and in doing so make what he'd done to the two men Finn had brought him look like a pampering. Vidar had claimed their best chance, despite his extensive armory, would be the element of surprise. To wait and strike when it seemed the very *last* thing they might do. So far his plan—and it had in no way dissipated with time, just patiently controlled in Vidar's disciplined way—had seemed to have potential. With each passing day, Vidar's elusiveness to the world spread word that he was probably dead. This, he had once shared with Finn, could indeed be the greatest plan of all—to be attacked by a dead man. Yet as long as Vidar truly lived, he *would* one day seek his vengeance against the Blue; of this Finn was certain, and he would *happily* stand at Vidar's side throughout, offering up his last dying breath if it came to that.

And so now, Finn mused, such a prospect might not be so far off. Especially if word—true or not; distinction between the two did not deter its speed of travel—spread as fast as it so often does. If Gash felt Finn was starting a war, was responsible for the disappearance of two of his men, or—worse yet—had delivered them to Vidar himself, then a time would soon come when his options were simple: run or fight.

And Finn did *not* like to run…as was made clear by the female voice behind him now, speaking the first words to Finn she'd done in years: "You know, for someone like you, you're really not that hard to find."

Finn recognized the voice immediately. *Sadie.*

He turned slowly in his seat. "Someone like me?"

"You'd think you'd take greater effort in keeping a low profile," she said.

Finn shook his head. "If I have something coming to me, I prefer to get it over with quickly."

"Yeah, I remember."

He fought a smirk. "I didn't hear any complaints from you at the time."

"You always fell asleep before I could."

Finn poured himself another shot. "What do you want?"

Sadie took a seat across from him. "Some of that whiskey would be nice."

Finn gestured to his glass. "Only got the one glass."

Sadie reached across the table and took it, downing the whiskey in one go. She then slid it back to him. "Encore," she said.

The smirk was getting harder to fight. Though he'd never admit it to a single soul, he'd been angry for a spell when Sadie up and left without a word a while back. And though he wasn't naïve enough to think the two of them were the partnering type, he *did* think they'd had a connection of sorts, a connection that at least warranted a goodbye. But time had now erased any bitterness he might have once had; all he saw before him was the hardened charm and beauty of the woman he'd all but fallen for, or as close to falling for as someone like Finn ever came.

Or maybe it was just the whiskey.

Finn filled the glass back up and slid it back to her. Sadie took it and downed it in one go again.

"So, you just came here to get drunk with me, is that it?" Finn asked her.

Sadie slid the empty glass back and gestured for a refill. "Can't I do both?"

"Depends." Finn poured her a shot and slid it back.

Sadie downed it. "Depends on what?"

"What the other half of 'both' is. Any chance it's what I hope it is?"

Sadie slid the glass back. "None."

"Can't blame a guy for trying." This time Finn filled the glass and took his own shot.

"Feel like telling me what happened with the two Blue members?" Sadie asked.

Finn shot a glance over at the bartender. Though he knew Sadie likely hadn't gotten her information from the man, it was chatty little worms of his ilk that happily spread "news" throughout the wastelands with all the merit of crap whiskey.

"Nothing to tell," Finn said, glancing back at her. "Chances are I heard what you heard."

"And what did I hear?"

Finn sighed. "If this banter we've got going was going to lead to something, I could chalk it all up to foreplay. But since you made it clear that's not going to happen, you'll forgive me if I ask you to get to your point."

Sadie smirked. "You always did speak your mind."

He gulped another shot and shrugged. "Not all of us can read them."

Sadie frowned and kicked the chair next to her. "You always spoke your mind, but you weren't an asshole."

Finn dropped his head for a moment, lifted it and said: "I'm sorry—I don't think anybody heard."

Sadie's frown remained. "I sure as hell hope not, because as I'm sure you already know, you and I share a similar problem."

Finn nodded. "Yeah, I heard. I'm surprised you're coming up for air so soon."

"Funny you used that choice of words."

thirty-three

Sadie told Finn everything. From killing the Blue gang member at the card table; to passing out on the side of the road shortly after; to the blind kid finding her; to getting in the blind kid's head, seeing some seriously messed-up stuff that made her linger too long and pass out again; to waking up below ground in a thriving community of moles. Good people. People who had saved her life and were trustworthy.

And most importantly, the tunnel within the community that ran smack below the Blue compound—a tunnel that the Blue knew absolutely nothing about.

"How do you know?" Finn asked.

"Common sense," Sadie replied. "You think if vermin like them knew that tunnel existed, they wouldn't have gone down there by now, wiped those poor people out?"

Finn nodded. "True."

Sadie then went on to explain about Dakota, once labeled Four. How it was only a matter of time until Gash figured out how one of his wenches, pregnant no less, slipped through his fingers. Only a matter of time until he found the tunnel that had been a mystery to him and his men all these years. And once he did…

"So, you were planning to head through this tunnel and then climb on up into the Blue compound and kill Gash on your own?" Finn asked, the whiskey forcing an almost condescending tone into his voice he would have otherwise suppressed. "You know how solid their base is?"

Sadie, her certain annoyance for his condescension instead rolling right off her back (whiskey was the supreme therapist in the wastelands), told him about how she'd planned to get the layout ahead of time, never intending to go in blind; how when Dakota came onto the scene, Sadie decided to get into her head as a way of accessing the ultimate blueprint, only to recoil in frustration at exactly what Finn had all but snorted at just now—how fortified the Blue compound truly was.

"I don't like running," Sadie began. "But I would have if it meant bringing attention away from these people who helped me. But now, with that pregnant kid having escaped? Guarantee the Blue have forgotten all about me. I'd be just a bonus if they found that tunnel, stormed on down there to reclaim Gash's prize, and found my sorry butt hiding out."

"So, the essence of your plan hasn't changed," Finn said. "Save your own butt or save the moles' butts, you still want to wipe out the Blue." Finn took another shot and winced from this one. He cleared whiskey from his throat with a few coughs into his fist, then added: "Except now you have to do it far sooner rather than later, with the added fun of knowing that pulling it off is going to be a million times harder than you originally thought."

Sadie took the bottle and poured herself a shot. Downed it and said: "If I could just get Gash alone somehow. He never leaves the compound, does he?"

Finn shook his head. "Most warlords rarely do. Besides, even if you killed Gash, you'd still have a whole mess of pissed-off Blue gunning for you."

"Doubt it," Sadie said. "You know how these idiots are. They're moths to Gash's flame. Put out the flame and they'll scatter aimlessly."

Finn did another shot, then ran a hand over his shaved head until his fingers arrived at a long white scar by the nape of his tanned neck. "My guess is you never heard about Wrath."

Sadie went to reach for the bottle but stopped halfway. "*Wrath?*"

"Gash's number one. Crazy as they get. Dude collects *teeth* around his neck. If you think a guy like that is just gonna scatter after Gash is dead…"

"*Wrath,*" Sadie said again. She resumed her reach for the bottle and poured herself another. "The names these idiots give themselves."

"His real name could be Sally for all we know," Finn said. "Doesn't change who he is. And that's a crazed killer." Finn rubbed his hand over his head, stopping on the scar again.

Sadie spotted the more-than-usual contempt in his recall, the now-twice gesture to the scar she already knew existed at the base of his scalp "You know him well, huh?" she asked, with not a little insinuation.

"Yeah—we tangled right after Sten was killed," he said.

"Too good?" she asked.

Finn frowned. "I'm here talking to you now, aren't I? If he was too good, I'd be too dead."

"So what happened?"

"Who cares? We're both alive, but we'd love nothing more than to see the other dead."

Sadie downed her drink. "Well, then maybe you'll like my proposition—and no, it's not what you're hoping it is, stud."

thirty-four

Finn once again found himself in Vidar's chambers. No gift-wrapped Blue members for Vidar to torture for days on end this time, but perhaps something better. A chance to eradicate the Blues indefinitely.

Finn relayed Sadie's backstory with the Blue, with the moles that helped her, and now with her plan to attack the Blue compound—hit from above to keep them occupied while more troops filed in from the mysterious tunnel below. Classic wartime strategy of misdirection.

"This martyr, she's the one you referred to earlier? The one you know intimately?" Vidar asked.

"I never admitted to that," Finn said.

Vidar smirked and said: "Do you trust her?"

"She has every reason to want the Blue wiped out as we do. Maybe not so much on a personal level, but she definitely wants them gone. That's good enough for me. But gun to my head, yes, I do trust her. Plus, she's grown fond of these people who've been helping her. She tries to act tough and indifferent when discussing them, but there's the subtlest of affection in her manner. I see it. She wants to ensure their safety."

Vidar turned his back on Finn and considered his words. The awesome V-shape to Vidar's back had Finn wondering whether Vidar's workout included pullups with ten motorhorses strapped to his waist.

Vidar turned back to Finn. "I would need to see the tunnel for myself," he said.

"Of course."

"If I find the plan doable, we do it my way, and *only* my way."

"Absolutely," Finn said.

Vidar approached Finn. Got close. The intensity in his icy blue eyes had Finn wanting to use the toilet, and he trusted Vidar with his life.

"Make it clear to everyone," Vidar began, "that Gash is to be mine and mine alone. My men will know this, but be sure your Sadie and her people do."

"I'll tell Sadie, but I'm quite sure her people won't be involved. They'll allow us access to the tunnel, but they aren't fighters. Chances are it'll be me, Sadie, and you and your men."

Vidar placed a powerful hand on Finn's shoulder. It felt like a bear's paw. "I cannot be clearer about this, Finn. Gash's soul is mine."

"I know, my friend," Finn said. "And if I could be so bold at a time like this to ask a favor of my own?"

Vidar's massive hand left Finn's shoulder only for him to now clamp both hands onto Finn's face, bunching his cheeks (and what felt like cheek *bones*) together as his demeanor oddly and suddenly shifted into a celebratory bark of laughter into Finn's scrunched face. Vidar did not need to hear Finn's favor to know what it was.

"The bastard is all yours," he told Finn, still—oddly, considering the blood-freezing intensity of his manner only seconds ago—grinning and chuckling occasionally. Perhaps it was the prospect of finally claiming his vengeance on Gash. Perhaps Vidar was crazier than Finn had ever thought he was. Perhaps Finn didn't give a shit as long as he and Vidar were on the same team.

"On one condition," Vidar then added.

"What's that?" Finn managed through mushed cheeks.

Vidar barked more laughter and released his hold on Finn's face. "I've heard the sick bastard is keen on necklaces. Promise me you'll remove what he has now and replace it with one of your own. The kind you can't take off…" Vidar made a slit-throat gesture across his own throat, *skkkrrrrt!* sound effect and all.

Finn said: "Done. I'll even make sure the necklace goes all the way around, not just the front."

Vidar cocked his head and splayed a hand, his gestures pure theatrics, his tone playful. "You do that, and the bastard's head might pop clean off, Finley!"

"Well, then I'd be doing his ugly ass a favor."

Though they were still deep in the chamber, Finn would have bet his legs Vidar's laughter that followed was echoing throughout the wastelands.

thirty-five

Teir and Koty sat on the couch together as she read to him from one of Rafa's books. *Through The Looking-Glass* was the title. It was one of a pair of stories about a girl named Alice that Rafa had read to him many years ago. Teir had enjoyed the books as a child and was pleased to find that he was enjoying them again, but in a totally new way. He was noticing details and puzzles and jokes in the text that he'd been too young to understand before. And Koty was a good reader. She didn't know all the big words like Rafa did and had to sound things out a few times, but she made up voices for each of the characters as if she was on stage acting in a one-person show. Teir found it extremely entertaining.

It was nice to be so pleasantly distracted. It was a needed break from his worrying about the long days that Rafa had been spending at the clinic treating patients with the Clear Sadie had found, coupled with the long stretches in his lab, studying the strange substance. Elixa assured Teir that Rafa was eating and sleeping enough, but Teir heard the exhaustion in her voice. He knew she was almost as driven as her grandson in their mission to heal the sick and guard the health of the community, so instead of being comforted by her promises, Teir just worried about her too.

And, of course, there was the fact that a deranged warlord and his gang of bloodthirsty thugs lived at the other end of the tunnel Teir had found. It was only a matter of time before they came knocking on the community's doors looking for Sadie and Koty. Teir and Koty *both* needed a break from worrying about that.

Teir hadn't known Koty for very long, but he liked her a lot. She didn't treat him carefully because of his poor vision like most other people did, and she was tough and smart. The past few years of her life had been sheer hell, but she didn't feel sorry for herself at all. She just felt grateful that she'd managed to escape into the arms of a community that would help her and the child she was carrying. She seemed to like Teir as well. She'd barely left his side since Sadie had looked inside Koty's mind, decided on the next course of action, and gone up above to find help. Koty had come right out and told Teir that she trusted him and Rafa, and would stay with them in their apartment while Sadie was gone. Then she'd made a joke about Teir's poor vision giving her an advantage if he tried anything improper. She sure knew how to make him laugh.

Fortunately, Sadie had found her friend Finn up above, and he had agreed to help them. Finn had in turn asked for help from a friend of his, a very powerful and mysterious man who had insisted on seeing the tunnel himself before he would agree to anything. Sadie and Izar had become a formidable team in directing the mission, and convincing the community elders to allow strangers to prowl around in remote parts of the complex had been tricky, but they'd ultimately succeeded.

That's where the two women were now, showing the tunnel to Finn and his friend, while Rafa worked tirelessly in the clinic, and Teir and Koty followed Alice on her adventures.

Koty read on, exaggerating the distress in the conversation perfectly: "'Only it is so *very* lonely here!' Alice said in a melancholy voice; and at the thought of her loneliness two large tears came rolling down her cheeks. 'Oh, don't go on like that!' cried the poor Queen, wringing her hands in despair. 'Consider what a great girl you are. Consider what a long way you've come to-day. Consider what o'clock it is. Consider anything, only don't cry!'"

Teir heard the apartment door open, and Koty stopped reading.

"Teir?"

It was Rafa.

"Yes?" Teir replied.

"There are some people here who want to meet you."

Teir stood up from the couch and approached the door as Rafa entered the room followed by about half a dozen people—Izar and Sadie and four men Teir didn't know. Rafa turned on the overhead light they rarely used because it was so bright and used too much electricity.

As light flooded the room, Teir immediately sensed tenseness in the murmurs and gasps from the four strangers. One of them, a towering giant with wild blond hair, stepped forward quickly and demanded to know who he was.

"I'm Teiresias."

"Who are your parents?" the man asked, a frantic edge to his voice.

"I…I don't know. Rafa found me in the desert when I was little."

The man demanded to see the skin on his back.

"*What?*" Teir said. "*Why?*"

The man stepped very close. Teir could feel his eyes studying him closely. "Is there a scar below your left shoulder?" the man asked. "The skin concave where a chunk of flesh was removed and the area numb to the touch?"

Teir felt as though ice had just flooded his veins. "Rafa, what's going on?"

"*Answer me!*" the man shouted.

Teir saw Rafa approach to help, but the huge man shoved him away and grabbed Teir by the shoulders—

—and in a fast and fluid series of moves Teir had practiced so many times they had become second nature, he used the big man's size and momentum to break the hold and send the man stumbling to his right, nearly toppling him. Had it not been for the tremendous size difference, the big man would have been flat on his back, no question.

"*Who the hell are you, and how do you know about that scar?!*" Teir yelled.

The man's reaction to this could not have been more bizarre or unexpected. After a moment's pause, during which no one made a sound, he began to laugh. Hard and loud like he had completely lost his mind. In between gasps for breath from laughing so hard, it sounded as though he was sobbing.

"Well, I'll be damned," said another man, clearly astonished. "I think we found Sten's boy."

thirty-six

His name was Brandr.

It *was*.

Now it was Teiresias; Brandr was the name his parents had given him. His parents, Sten and Runa. He'd also had a little sister named Tyra, who had adored him and followed him everywhere from the moment she could walk.

And this grief-crazed mountain of a man who knew about the strange old scar on his back, and who was going to help Sadie and her friend Finn annihilate the community's dangerous neighbors above…this man was his grandfather Vidar.

And those neighbors above were the people who had murdered his family.

They had tried to murder him too, but somehow Teir had escaped into the desert.

It was an awful lot of information to process, but Teir did his best to stay calm and brave as he sat across the dining table from Vidar, listening to detailed accounts of his early life and of his family's brutal and agonizing death.

For as long as he could remember, he had wanted to know who he was and where he'd come from. What he'd seen upon meeting Sadie and experiencing her gift had only intensified his desire. But now that it was all being told to him at once, in an emotional torrent from the only other person alive who was as affected by the tragedy as Teir, it was almost more than he could handle. Almost, but not quite; his adoptive family had raised him well.

Vidar asked a lot of questions, too, about where and how and in what condition Teir had been found, and Rafa did his best to answer them all. At first Teir was uncomfortable with all the details of his sad past being discussed in such detail in front of strangers, but after a while even he was impressed with the fact of his own survival and of the young man he'd become. Mostly he was proud of and grateful to Rafa for taking such good care of him for the past eight years.

"So how did I get the scar on my back?" Teir asked Vidar.

"You were attacked by a wild dog when you were very small," his grandfather told him.

"It bit me?"

"It tried to *eat* you."

"Why?"

Vidar chuckled. "I imagine because it was hungry."

"So why *didn't* it eat me?"

"Because your own dog tore its throat out before the beast could do more harm to you."

"*My* dog?"

"Yes."

Teir squinted, as if it would help him see into the past. "What was its name?"

"Otto."

Teir smiled as the sound of the name brought forth a rush of memories, and a door in his mind that had been locked for many years was thrown wide open. He recalled the dog's smooth fur and powerful body, the smell of his breath, the slimy wetness of his tongue when he licked Teir's face, the way he looked directly into your eyes when you spoke to him, like he understood every word.

Teir could see him clearly.

"A big white dog with pale blue eyes," Teir said quietly.

"You remember him?" Vidar asked.

"I do. I remember waking him once from a sound sleep and being scared half to death when he jumped up and barked at me."

His grandfather started laughing again, the sound of which Teir decided he really liked even though it was startlingly loud.

"You learned quickly never to do *that* again," Vidar told him.

Teir nodded, his smile broadening as the scene replayed in his mind like it had happened only last week. "He was deaf, wasn't he?"

"Yes he was," Vidar said. "When you began to have trouble with your vision he became even more attached to you. As if he knew that the two of you could navigate the world better together than separately. He was a fiercely intelligent creature."

Teir's smile faded as a thought occurred to him, and he had to ask. "What happened to him? When the Blue took us?"

There was a moment of heavy silence before his grandfather answered.

"He died trying to protect the people he loved."

Another moment of silence followed.

Then Vidar spoke again. "Enough talk; there'll be plenty of time for this later." His grandfather's huge hand covered Teir's where it rested on the table, and the man squeezed gently. "Right now we have a war to win…and brutal vengeance to exact upon those who took so much from us. Are you with me, my boy?"

"Yes, sir," Teir replied. "I'm with you."

thirty-seven

The meeting was held in North Hall. A big round room with a big round table. The lighting, as was the case throughout the community, was low to conserve energy, but more than sufficient.

Seated along the perimeter of the round table were Vidar and a few of his more experienced soldiers. Next to Vidar sat Teir (at *both* their insistence), and next to Teir sat Koty (her intimate knowledge of the compound her ticket for attendance). The remainder of the circle held Sadie, Finn, Izar, and Julen.

Absent were Rafa and Elixa. They remained in the clinic, healing the sick with the newfound Clear. As much a necessity as they believed a war with the Blue was, they wanted no part in planning one. They were healers, not fighters.

Sadie continued to marvel at the size of Vidar, and she was finding that his manner rivaled his physique. Every word, every gesture crackled with power. Perhaps, Sadie mused, more so now at the discovery of his long-thought-dead grandson. Yes, it was almost assuredly so. And Sadie had known her kiddo Teir long enough by now to see a change in his manner as well. A seemingly new air of maturity that shone in his tone and posture. And why not? After the hell the kid had been through, wandering aimlessly in that tortured head of his, to then finally discover that you were the grandson of a titan like Vidar? Talk about reparations, baby.

The details of the attack on the Blue remained fairly straightforward, the tunnel Teir had discovered being the key: The attack from above, while strong and true, would serve as a decoy while Vidar and more of his men filed in from below, hitting them obliquely and with great surprise. Finn had expressed his insistence on settling his score with Wrath personally (Sadie then leaning into Finn's ear and whispering how tough and scary he was), to which Vidar instantly agreed, with the table's similar understanding that General Gash was to be his and his alone (Finn then leaning into Sadie's ear and suggesting she say the same to Vidar. She did not).

Bumps in the meeting first came with the discussion of walling off the tunnel. Vidar dismissed the idea instantly.

"Sound in theory," he said, "but logistically unrealistic."

Sadie, while warming less and less to the idea of walling off the tunnel after Koty had escaped and time was no longer on their side, still wanted to hear Vidar's rationale and, more importantly, his alternative for protecting the community.

"Understand," she began, "my idea for walling off the tunnel was imagined when I believed I could enter the Blue compound on my own. This was before Koty"—Sadie gestured towards the pregnant girl—"had escaped, and time was our ally. But I know now that we don't *have* time. When Gash and his men finish scouring the wastelands looking for Koty, it won't be long before they start scouring within. Discovering the entrance to the tunnel seems an unfortunate probability, wouldn't you say?"

"I would say," Vidar said.

A pause at the table.

Macho asshole, Sadie thought. *Is he so confident in wiping out the Blue that he believes prophylactic measures in protecting the community just in case are unnecessary?*

Sadie splayed her hands. "Okay…well, then, with all due respect, what are the members of this community to do if members of the Blue slip past us in battle and find their way down into the tunnel?"

Vidar leaned back in his chair. "Are you aware of what I do for a living, girl?"

"*Sadie.*"

Vidar closed his eyes, smiled, and held up an apologetic hand. "Are you aware of what I do for a living, Sadie?"

"Only if rumors count."

"My chief occupation is as an arms dealer. In the absence of legitimate firepower throughout our land, I am a reliable, albeit expensive, source of true weaponry. Needless to say, in our case, price will be no object."

Sadie splayed her hands again, decided to voice her previous thoughts no matter how confrontational it sounded. "Okay, but then what? You're saying our firepower will be so great that wiping out the Blue is all but certain? That fallback measures for protecting this community are unnecessary?"

Vidar boomed with laughter. Julen flinched.

"Oh, Sadie, even *I* am not so arrogant as to ensure victory," he said. "No, what I am proposing is building a wall of a different sort at the tunnel entrance." Vidar looked over at Izar. "You are the one in charge of security within your community?"

Izar nodded once. "I am, yes."

"Ever fired a Gatling gun?"

A small smile crept along the corner of Izar's mouth. "No, I haven't."

Vidar winked at Izar and then returned to Sadie. "I much prefer a wall of bullets to that of stone."

thirty-eight

"I'm not sure I follow," Sadie said.

"It's rather simple," Vidar replied. "Izar here and an army of my men will stand guard at the tunnel entrance...with enough firepower to blow them to pieces should any manage to slip through."

Sadie frowned, hesitated, and then finally said: "And how long will Izar and your men stand guard? Days? Weeks? *Years?*"

Now it was Vidar who frowned. "I'm not sure I follow *you.*"

Sadie sat back in her chair. "Look, I'm all about optimism and morale, but let's weigh every option here. Suppose we go to war and get our butts kicked. You, me, Finn, none of us come out of that compound alive. What then? Are Izar and your men expected to stand guard at the tunnel entrance with your metaphorical wall of firepower indefinitely?"

"A fair point," Vidar said. "If such a thing should happen, we will collapse the tunnel."

Julen, quiet up until this point in the meeting, leaned forward in his chair. "Collapse the tunnel?"

"Indeed," Vidar said. "A much faster method than all that brick and mortar, if you ask me."

Sadie and Julen exchanged a look.

Sadie said: "Let me get this straight; you're saying if our luck runs out, and we die up there, then Izar and your men blow the tunnel up?"

"Correct," was all Vidar said.

Now Sadie and Izar shared a look.

Sadie said: "You're awfully cavalier about such a plan. Isn't that dangerous to the community? What about the blowback?"

Vidar laughed. "Have you *seen* the tunnel? It goes on for damn near miles." He placed a hand on Teir's shoulder and squeezed, beaming down at him as he spoke. "How my grandson made it in as far as he did is nothing short of astounding." He kept his hand on Teir but brought his attention back to Sadie. "The explosives will be placed by the hatch leading into the entrance of the Blue compound. Once it blows, the only way into this community of yours will be from above, and that's certainly hidden well enough. These people would have nothing to fear."

"Fine," Sadie said. "Let's say blowback is minimal. The entrance to the compound by way of the hatch is destroyed, and the debris from the explosion gives us an instant roadblock. How do you plan on rigging the whole thing without us triggering it prematurely?"

"My men—all of us—will be equipped with military radios. This will allow us to keep you updated on what's going on above, in addition to alerting Izar and my men down here to any gang members who might have slipped by us and are heading their way." He looked at Izar and winked again. "That's when Izar here will get to try her hand with a Gatling gun."

Izar nodded back but did not smile as she'd done before; the reality of such a likely prospect approaching ever faster clearly triggering some sort of adrenaline release within her. Brave and lacking naught in heart, Izar's combat experience up until now had never been battle-tested. That was about to change.

Vidar went on. "And should one of us, for whatever reason, see fit to head back through the tunnel before the war is done, well, then our radios should be quite handy in avoiding any unnecessary casualties, yes? Wouldn't want Izar to have any fun with the Gatling gun at *my* expense!" He barked out a single laugh.

"So, the word to go ahead and blow the tunnel as a last resort will be given via radio," Sadie said.

"Correct."

"And you talk clearly when you're dead, do you?" Sadie asked.

Vidar's laughter boomed like sudden music. "You're very quick, Sadie. Finn always did have good taste in women."

Finn immediately opened his mouth to object, but Vidar went on.

"The signal to blow the hatch will not be given verbally," he said. "My men will check in with us periodically. If they lose touch and begin to worry, they will send out a distress signal, urging us to respond."

"Distress signal?"

One of Vidar's men produced two of the handheld radios and placed them on the table. Vidar took one and clicked a switch along the radio's edge. A small red light began flashing on the surface of the second radio.

"If my men have not heard from us in a while, and fear the worst, they will trigger this distress signal. If we are alive and see it, we are to respond within an agreed-upon period of time that we are still alive and to *not* blow the tunnel."

"And if we're alive, but deep in battle, unable to respond?"

"Every one of us—those going into the compound from above and those from below—will be equipped with a radio. Someone *will* see it and respond."

"One more thing," Sadie said.

"Oh good, I was beginning to think you intended to leave a stone unturned."

"This explosive you intend to place in the tunnel," Sadie said. "What's to stop your men from accidentally shooting it should members of the Blue slip by us and work their way down into the tunnel? You talk about unleashing a wall of firepower. Suppose a stray bullet clips that explosive?"

"The explosive will be placed up and inside the hatch. The odds of a stray bullet catching the device, even if we are being gratuitous with our ammunition—and we *will be* gratuitous—are miniscule."

"What about lights?" Sadie asked.

"What about them?"

"Well, surely a man with your means could acquire high-powered lights to penetrate the black of the tunnel. It could increase our accuracy *and* momentarily blind any Blue that slipped through, doubling our advantage."

"Hard to argue with such logic. But a sudden light may induce panic fire. We want to hit them before they even *realize* they're in a firefight. We *use* the darkness to our advantage."

Sadie didn't reply. Just sat back in her chair, silent.

"My word!" Vidar said with a big grin. "I think I've finally satisfied her! Nothing *you* could ever say, yes, Finn?"

Again Finn leaned forward to object. This time it was Julen who cut him off.

"Why do the two of you talk as if we have no say in the matter?" he said.

All heads turned towards Julen.

"What matter are you referring to?" Vidar asked.

"*All of it*," Julen said. "My understanding was that this meeting was to be a *discussion* as to what was best for the community. I've seen no evidence of that. Only logistics concerning an attack plan that I have *yet* to give my okay to."

Vidar sat back in his chair and sighed.

Izar rubbed her father's shoulder. "This is something we must do, Dad. Do you sit and wait for the rattlesnake to bite before you bite *it*?"

"There are many ways to deal with a rattlesnake that don't involve violence, Izar," Julen said.

"Yes, there are. But we are not in a position to indulge any of them. Our only other option than what we've been discussing thus far is to run. Is that what you want? To leave all this behind?" She waved a hand over the room. "Live as nomads when we have so diligently worked within our community to do anything but?"

Vidar leaned forward. "There's nothing wrong with running, Julen. Contrary to what you might think about me, I suggest flight just as often as fight if the circumstances dictate flight as the best course of action. I am not a mindless brute with a lust for war. Unlike that fool above our heads, I am a *true* general who weighs his options carefully, and then proceeds with the most efficient course of action, be it run, hide, or fight.

"As your daughter has already said, if you wish to save your community, save all you've worked for and attained over the years, then your only alternative is to, as your daughter so aptly put it, bite the rattlesnake first. And make no mistake, Julen; what you have above your head are rattlesnakes. Mean and nasty and plentiful. And like most rattlesnakes, we cannot avoid being bitten by simply leaving them be. They are looking for her—" He pointed at Koty. "Looking for *us*. Your daughter is correct. We must bite first."

Julen still looked hesitant. Izar took his hand in hers.

"Do you trust me, Dad?" she asked him.

"Of course."

"Do you believe I have the community's best interests at heart? That our safety is everything to me?"

"I do, yes."

"Then please keep that trust here and now. These men above us, they are horrible men. Savages who will, given the chance, come down here and do great harm to us all. They have no morals or code of honor. Women and children are not off limits to them. Consider what they did to Koty and her friends. To Teir's mother and sister. To *Teir*."

Teir's hand resting on the table became a fist. Vidar wrapped his massive hand over it and gave it a squeeze.

"I don't want anyone in our community involved in battle," Julen said.

"The only involvement will be to heal the wounded," Izar said. "You know Rafa and Elixa will spearhead that. Only Teir and I will be at the tunnel entrance to stand with Vidar's men."

"*Teir*? Why Teir?" Julen asked.

Teir started to say something, but Izar held up a hand.

"It is Teir's wish, and therefore Vidar's wish," was all she said.

Julen looked over at Vidar. Vidar's return gaze was ice, held no chance for debate.

He turned back to Izar and nodded. "Okay."

Vidar pushed back his chair and stood. "Okay! I propose we break for food and rest and then meet back here in one hour; we have much strategy to discuss." He glanced over at Julen. The uncertainty in Julen's face had lightened, but only somewhat. "Julen," Vidar began, "while only a fool ensures victory, what I *can* tell you is that I have been waiting for an opportunity like this for a very long time." He looked down at Teir, rubbed his shoulder, and then glanced back up at Julen. "I do *not* intend to let it go to waste."

thirty-nine

Sadie knocked on Rafa and Teir's apartment door, said, "Heads up—coming in," and then entered.

Teir was sitting on the sofa by himself. He looked bothered.

"Hey, kiddo," Sadie said. "Where's Rafa?"

"At the clinic. He and Elixa are still treating people with Clear."

Sadie flopped next to him on the couch. "Was gonna tell him how the meeting went," she said.

"I can tell him."

"Yeah, but he doesn't like to talk about that stuff with you, does he?"

Teir frowned. "What do you mean?"

"War stuff. Fighting."

Teir shrugged. "No, I guess not."

"That's what Izar's for, right?" Sadie asked.

"I guess."

"Doesn't she train with you? Talk fighting and all that?"

Teir nodded. "Yeah…"

"But…?"

"She holds back sometimes. On Rafa's account maybe. Or maybe because she tires faster than I do. I don't know."

An uncomfortable pause.

Sadie groaned. "Okay, this tiptoeing around the issue thing is making my brain hurt. Be a man and tell me whatever the hell is on your mind or I'm leaving," she said.

"Go then," he said.

"I will."

"Then do it."

"I am."

Another pause.

Sadie shoved Teir on the shoulder. "Would you just talk?"

He swatted her hand away. "Get off!"

"Tell me what the hell's wrong."

"*I wanna fight!*" he blurted.

"What?"

"Alongside my grandfather," he said.

Sadie expected it might be this. "He's letting you stand guard at the gate with Izar and his men, right? All logic would say you shouldn't, that you should be back in the community with the others."

"Why, because I'm a kid? Because I can't see well?"

"Yes and yes."

Teir hammered his fist down on the sofa cushion.

"Look, you can't help the fact that you're a *kid*," she said. "You'll grow with time. And judging by the size of your grandfather, you'll grow into a freaking mountain."

"And my sight?" he said.

"Can't help you with that one," she said. "But I've felt your strength. You get your hands on someone your size, and they're going for a ride."

"And that's the extent of it, isn't it?" he said. "Judo."

"What the hell's judo?" Sadie asked.

"It's the primary martial art that Izar and I train in together. It relies on grip and leverage to unbalance the opponent, using their weight and momentum against them."

"Sounds perfect for you."

"There's no striking in judo. No weapons."

"She won't teach you that stuff?" Sadie asked.

Teir shook his head. "And why should she? You can't hit what you can't see, right?"

Sadie groaned again. "No, no, no—*I'm* the martyr here, not you. None of this 'feel sorry for me' crap."

Teir grumbled under his breath.

"Look, I'm a thirty-five-year-old female rogue who wanders the wastelands. The fact that I'm still alive defies all logic."

"You're a martyr," Teir said flatly.

"So?"

"And you can shoot a gun."

Sadie frowned. "There are times when I can't use a gun *or* my gift, and I've still managed okay for a hundred-and-twenty-pound woman."

Teir snorted. "I'm not *that* blind."

"You want my help or not?"

"I'm not really sure what you're offering."

Sadie stood. "Stand up," she said.

Teir did.

"We're about the same height," she said. She then stood on the couch and guided Teir in front of her by the shoulders. "Now I've got nearly a foot on you."

"Your boobs are in my face."

She gave his head a harmless swat. "Shut up and close your eyes."

"Why? I need all the help I can get," he said.

"If you can do this with your eyes closed, then any visual impairment becomes irrelevant, yes?"

"I guess."

"Good. Close your eyes."

He did.

"Think you can find my ear?" she asked.

"Huh?"

"The things I hear with. Think you can reach up and touch one of them?"

Teir reached up and placed a hand over her ear.

"Good. Now press your thumb into my eye. Gently, please."

Sadie closed her eye. Teir placed his thumb on it and pressed lightly.

"If you can find my ear, you can find my eyes. Do it with both hands now."

Teir reached up with both hands, placed them over Sadie's ears, and then pushed both thumbs gently into her eyes.

"Good," Sadie said. "Keep your eyes shut. Think you can find my butt?"

"*What?*"

"Pretend I'm Koty. Think you can find my butt?"

Teir wrinkled his nose but eventually placed a hand on one of her butt cheeks. Sadie withdrew a knife from her waist and placed it in Teir's other hand. "Place that blade a few inches below my butt, against the back of my leg. Against the hamstring. You slice deep into that and he's not walking anytime soon. Never mind the pain. You can find the butt, you can find the hamstring."

Sadie spotted the tiniest of smiles begin to creep onto Teir's face.

"Keep your eyes closed. Now comes my personal favorite. Put the knife down and then put your hands on my hips."

Teir did.

"I'm personally not equipped with them, but you are," Sadie said. "Wanna guess where I'm going with this?"

Teir succumbed to the smile.

"Knife 'em, strike 'em, or squeeze 'em for all you're worth. Up to you. They're all a good time."

His smile grew.

"You can find his ear, you can find his eyes. You can find his butt, you can find his hamstring. You can find his hips, you can find his twig and berries."

Teir barked out a laugh and then quickly caught himself.

Sadie hopped off the couch. "I think that's enough for today," she said. "Feel better?"

"A little," he replied, remnants of the smile and laughter lingering on his face.

Too cool for a full-on yes, Sadie thought. *But I'll take it.* "Wanna get something to eat?" she asked.

He shrugged. "Okay."

They went to the café and split a plate of bugs Sadie couldn't pronounce.

forty

The tavern's batwing doors flew open, and four commoners entered—laughing, grinning, carrying on. Most men, after indulging in sex and booze, left the tavern in such a boisterous state; few entered that way. To enter in such a state was to give your hand away. Show everyone in the tavern with half a brain that you had something to be happy about, something valuable—something that could be taken away, the means lethal more often than not.

This reality was especially true in this particular tavern. For it was a favorite spot of the Blue.

The four men took a table.

The waiter—a bald, thin man holding a circular tray—approached. "What'll it be, gentlemen?" he asked.

"Enough whiskey to drown a horse," one of them said, and the table broke out laughing.

"Celebrating, are you?" the waiter asked.

"You might say that," another said. "Unless you think getting your hands on a martyr is something to be sad about."

"I…I beg your pardon?" the waiter stammered.

"Ah duh…ah duh…" another mocked.

The table roared again.

"Just bring that whiskey," the first one said.

The waiter left.

.   .   .

The waiter, behind the bar now cleaning glasses, was approached. He glanced up and flinched when he spotted the blue colors on the hardened man before him.

"Those four men at the table over there," Knox, the Blue member, said. "Who are they?"

"No idea," the waiter said. "Get you a drink?"

Knox ignored him. "We heard them mention a martyr. What was that about?"

The waiter glanced back into the corner of the tavern where the remaining two members of the Blue sat, then replied in a whisper. "Said they'd gotten their hands on a martyr."

"What else?"

"That was all."

Knox just stared at him.

"I swear, that was all."

Knox glanced over his shoulder at the table of four men. They were drinking whiskey and grinning and laughing like fools. *Fools* being the key word. To blurt their supposed find of a martyr, and then to carry on as they were? Why not just stand on a table and announce you've found a map to one hell of a pocket of Clear, and then drape that map over your shoulder for all to see? They'd be lucky to be killed quickly.

Still, the claim of hoarding a martyr was big talk indeed. And if it were true, who knew where the hell they were keeping it? More importantly, who knew whether it was *the* martyr Knox's general was looking for? The one who'd killed one of their own and who was possibly in cahoots with Finn and Vidar—hell, maybe even responsible for the disappearance of The General's pregnant wench? Rumors had quickly spread throughout the compound; he knew the theories floating around.

"Send them over another bottle on us," Knox told the waiter.

.   .   .

The waiter brought over another bottle of whiskey and placed it on the table before the four men. "From the table in back," he said.

All four heads swiveled to get a look. A table of three rough-looking men—sporting denim and chains, scars, and, most noticeably, the color blue—raised their glasses toward the table of four.

The table of four raised theirs back.

"That was nice of them," one of the four said.

"What's with all the blue?" another asked. "They in a gang or something?"

The waiter could only shake his head and leave. Such naïveté in the wastelands was tough to stomach.

forty-one

The four men exited the tavern as they'd entered—flinging open the batwing doors with big grins and laughter.

And three new friends dressed in blue.

Knox had gotten exactly what he wanted from the four fools. After much whiskey, the fools had confirmed that they did indeed have a martyr stowed away somewhere close by; the martyr was a woman (and this had come as a pleasant surprise, though there was no certainty, of course, that she was *the* female martyr his general was looking for); and, best of all, the fools had agreed to take their three new friends dressed in blue to go see their prize. How these four men had survived as long as they had was a mystery to Knox.

.　　.　　.

The four men led them toward the outskirts of town, away from buildings of commerce, and toward scattered shacks that were a common sight throughout the perimeters of functioning towns. Shacks like these held all sorts of purposes. A place to sleep one off after too much booze. A place to take the flesh of your choice if you didn't want to give a tavern accommodation money for something that would take all of a few minutes. A place to hide yourself. Or, better still, a place to hide some*one*.

"I don't see but one more shack in the distance," Knox said to the four in front. "I'm hoping that's it?" He shot glances at Zane and Cruz, the other two members of the Blue's three. Both men frowned back in agreement. It was taking too long. The four were leading them too far.

But these fools? Knox thought. To think they'd be orchestrating some type of ambush was laughable. No, these four were simply doing as any would after mining treasure—burying it safely away. The question was, if the fools confirmed that the martyr was in fact tied up in that final shack in the distance, did they take them out now, or wait for visual confirmation? There always was the slight chance that these men did *not* have a martyr. They were gullible idiots, after all. For all they knew, they'd traded a large sum with nomads (so their story went as to how they'd acquired the martyr) for an ordinary woman. Nomads were as helpless to cheating a sucker as any gang member. More so.

"Yeah, that's the one," one of the four said with a grin. "We wanted to hide her as far from town as possible."

Yes, Knox's instinct had been correct. They had tucked their treasure safely away as most would. And had it not been for their unbelievable stupidity and big mouths (a greater cocktail for suicide, Knox didn't know), they might have been alive in the morning to reap the rewards of that treasure.

Knox gave a subtle but reassuring nod to his two comrades. *Patience,* the nod said.

They arrived at the shack. It was a decent enough size compared to most, but that was its only selling point; the exterior was a weather-beaten eyesore.

"Go on in," one of the four said with an eager smile.

A sudden feeling of unease came over Knox, his previous thoughts returning to him: *How these four men had survived as long as they had was a mystery…*

Shit. Had *they* been the gullible ones all along? Had this all been a ruse? Akin to the rumors floating around the compound as to how Finn had done something similar to two of theirs not long ago? Delivered them to *Vidar*?

The door of the shack opened. Finn stepped out. All three Blue members' mouths dropped open.

"What the hell's taking so long?" Finn said. "It's a freaking oven in there."

Knox summoned his dwindling courage. One on one, he could never take Finn. But he, Zane, and Cruz? They had a chance. And if the four who led them here were as skilled in combat as they were gullible, then he, Zane, and Cruz stood a solid chance.

Except they're not *gullible,* a sudden, frightening thought flew at him. *They led you right to* Finn, *you idiot. Who the hell are these guys?*

"What the hell is this?" Knox asked. He spun and faced the four men. "Who the hell are you guys?" Spinning back to Finn. "What's any of this got to do with you, Finn?" Back to the four. "Need Finn to fight your battles, do you?"

And then more insistent thoughts penetrated his rambling: *Fight what battles? Why the hell was Finn here lying in wait?? Who the hell are these guys??? What the hell is going on???*

Finn took a step out of the doorway. He smiled. "Trust me, these guys do *not* need me to fight their battles for them."

Knox looked at the four men. Their gullible, ignorant grins were gone. In their place was a collective expression of stone.

"Remember, don't kill them," Finn casually said to the four. "We need them alive."

Zane pulled a knife and rushed first. One of the four drew his own blade, parried Zane's thrust, and counter sliced him across the wrist, causing Zane to instantly drop his blade and cry out. The man then followed up with a heavy elbow to the hinge of Zane's jaw and Zane dropped, fast asleep.

Knox and Cruz exchanged a frantic look. They spun to flee, but were easily caught and put to sleep as quickly and deftly as their comrade.

Finn laughed at the aftermath of the fray. "I've had farts last longer," he said.

Vidar's men laughed too.

Finn flicked his chin over his shoulder towards the shack. "Come on, let's get them inside. We gotta do this quickly, and I'm not real keen on doing it, if you know what I mean."

Vidar's men grunted in agreement. Strapping explosives to a group of men's bare balls, while *highly* effective in creating obedience, was not a good time.

forty-two

"General," Wrath said, his eye in one of Gash's telescopes, looking down on the dusty courtyard of the compound from above. "You might want to come have a look at this."

Gash remained in his throne. "What is it I need to see that you can't tell me?"

Wrath turned toward Gash, an odd look of concern on his hardened face. "Three of ours entering the compound with four men and a woman."

"*What?*" Gash stood, shoved Wrath aside, and placed his good eye in the lens of the scope. He saw three of his men—Knox and…he did not remember the names of the other two—entering the main gate of the compound. Behind them were exactly what Wrath had described: four men—hardy-looking; not nomads or drunks—and a woman. The woman was bound at the wrists behind her back. One of the four men kept a firm hold on her elbow.

Gash pulled his eye from the lens and stomped out onto the balcony of his quarters with Wrath close behind. Both hands firm on the balcony's railings, he bellowed down into the belly of the compound's courtyard like a dictator to his minions.

"*Do I even need to ask?!*" he yelled.

Knox and the two others he could not recall froze, the four men leading the cuffed woman freezing behind them. The main gate closed behind all of them.

One of the four men, the one with his grip on the woman, looked up toward the balcony and spoke. "We come with a gift for you, General Gash."

"Hold your tongue, boy, or I will hold it for you." Gash brought his attention back to the bulk of his men littering the courtyard. "*Someone answer me!*"

No one spoke.

Gash hammered his meaty fist onto the balcony railing. "*Someone tell me why five strangers are inside MY compound without my say!*"

Knox glanced back toward the man with the woman, then up at his general. He fidgeted with his groin. His voice was uneasy. "She's the martyr, General," he said. "The one who gunned down one of ours."

The raw anger in Gash remained, but it was not so raw as to deny curiosity. "Is she then?"

The man with the supposed martyr spoke again. "That's right, General. We found her."

"And you are?"

The man shrugged. "Nobody important. We intended to keep the martyr for ourselves—to use her. But when we got word of what she'd done to one of yours, we figured you might be keen on having her."

"Having her for a price, you mean," Gash said.

The man shrugged again. "Of course."

"I am keen on having her, yes, but I am not one to compensate fools, boy."

The man frowned. "I'm sorry?"

"Did you honestly believe you could enter my compound with such a prize and expect to be compensated when I can simply *take* her from you?"

The man pulled the woman against his front as a shield. Pulled a gun from his waist and pressed it to her head. "You and I both know how priceless martyrs are, General. Even you're not brazen enough to do anything to risk her life."

Gash hammered his fist onto the balcony railing again. "*And he's armed, no less!!!*" He cast his furious gaze down towards the men guarding the main gate. "*Why were these men not searched upon entry?!*" He hammered his fist onto the railing yet again, nearly cracking the wood. "*Why were they even allowed entry?!*"

"They were with Knox and Zane and Cruz," one of his men at the gate replied sheepishly. "They vouched for them."

Gash shot his furious gaze towards Knox, who continued to shift uneasily where he stood. Before he could address Knox, the man with the woman spoke again. And to Gash's incredulity, his words were commands.

"*You—*" His forearm still around the woman, the man gestured with the gun for Knox to head toward the far end of the compound. "Over there."

General Gash watched in disbelief as Knox began to move.

The man with the woman turned to both Zane and Cruz now. "*You two—*" He gestured with the gun for Zane and Cruz to head back toward the gate. "Over there."

Zane and Cruz obeyed.

The remaining members of the Blue looked on, periodically exchanging glances with one another, blatantly confused at their fellow members' willingness to obey without pause.

Gash was physically sick with rage.

The man pressed the gun back to the woman's head. "If anyone tries anything, General, I *will* kill your prize."

Gash slapped both hands against the railing and leaned forward. Veins in his thick neck stood out like purple wiring. "You put too much faith in your bargaining chip, boy. I have had many martyrs in my day."

"One who gunned down one of your men in cold blood?" the man replied.

"And so I kill her now and get my vengeance," Gash said. "Find another martyr to play with. Where does that leave you and your men now, boy?"

The man swallowed hard. Looked over his shoulder at the other three.

Gash's rage became a malevolent grin.

"Take the girl, then," the man said. "We ask nothing in return but our lives."

Gash glanced back at Wrath. "I do love it when they beg."

The woman suddenly dropped to her knees, pressed her face into the man's thigh and began pleading gibberish as though the man actually had a say in the matter of her life.

"What's your plan, General?" Wrath asked.

Fingers thrumming along the balcony railing, Gash said: "Decisions, decisions…"

forty-three

During their second meeting back in the community, Sadie had told everyone that she would need roughly five minutes inside the Blue compound to use her gift and get a decent outlay of where the majority of guards were positioned, both on the grounds and within its walls.

Now, after gaining access to the Blue compound via the front gate (Finn had been correct; it was astounding just how mutinous the three members of the Blue would be with explosives rigged to their family jewels), Vidar's men had done a decent job of buying her those five minutes without incident.

And those five minutes had been more than enough.

Kneeling now against one of Vidar's men, seemingly pleading into his leg, she was telling Finn, Vidar, and Vidar's men exactly where each one of the Blue members was stationed within the compound via the radio stitched inside the pant leg of Vidar's man.

Everyone including General Gash and Wrath.

All Vidar and Finn had to do next was wait for the signal.

·   ·   ·

"General?" Wrath said.

Gash continued thrumming his fingers along the railing, his grin now a victorious smirk. He looked down at the four helpless fools and the martyr and considered his options. A glutton deciding on which culinary delight to indulge in first.

"The four men are stupid but appear fit. To take them for labor would be risky. The martyr, of course, I will take," Gash said.

"Shall I head down and do it personally, General?"

Gash glanced back at Wrath with a sly smirk. "Fancy eight more teeth around your neck, is that it?"

Wrath returned his toothless grin.

Gash brought his gaze back down below and spoke with his back to Wrath once again. "The four fools won't be the only ones to suffer today. Knox and those other two idiots need a lesson or two on loyalty, wouldn't you say?"

"And those who opened the gate without your say," Wrath added.

"True. But they were taking Knox and the other two at their word. If I punished all idiocy within my compound, I would be gazing down at a barren yard."

Wrath snorted.

The man with the martyr called up to Gash. "We're waiting, General."

Gash laughed and slapped the railing, looking back at Wrath once again. "The *nerve* on this one!"

.   .   .

Sadie got to her feet.

From the corner of his mouth, Vidar's man said: "We good?"

From the corner of her mouth, Sadie replied: "We're good."

Vidar's man brought his attention back to the balcony. "You know what, General?" he began. "I think we've changed our mind. I think we're just going to keep the martyr."

General Gash's victorious smile above did not change. "Oh, *are* you now?!" he called down.

Vidar's man smiled back. To the onlookers in the dark, his smile appeared inexplicably more victorious than Gash's.

Knox certainly thought so. He instantly clutched his groin with both hands and cried out: "*NO!!!*"

Sadie pulled both wrists free from her just-for-show binds and drew the small detonator from her waist. "I got something for that itch," she said.

· · ·

A series of three explosions above shook the tunnel below. Dust and debris fell from the open hatch. The ladder they'd brought for entry through the hatch rattled on its legs.

Vidar—his men in a line behind him, armed and ready for war—gripped the rails of the ladder and looked over at Finn with frightening intensity. "Leave no heart beating."

forty-four

Sadie hit the detonator.

Knox, still screaming, both hands still clamped over his groin in a feeble attempt at protection, exploded by the walls of the compound, taking several Blue members with him.

At the gate, Zane and Cruz fared no better. They too exploded the moment Sadie had hit the detonator, the impact so great it did not merely blow the giant door open, it blew the door *down*, this explosion too taking several Blue members in its blast.

Chaos reigned in the compound. Blue members momentarily froze with confusion. Even Gash and Wrath looked down from above in disbelief as fire and smoke filled the courtyard.

Vidar had counted on this. His men took this momentary advantage of shock and drew their concealed weapons, firing and slashing at anything blue that moved.

The Blue began regaining their wits, began fighting back. Amongst the billowing black smoke and blazing mounds of fire, gunshots rang out. Blind shots firing in all directions.

The Blue, from sheer numbers against Vidar's four who'd initially entered, began regaining the advantage. One of Vidar's four was hit in the chest. The Blue member who'd hit him followed him to the ground and slashed his throat, finishing it.

Blazing mounds of fire from the explosions were as strong as ever, but the black smoke was beginning to thin, offering more visibility, offering the Blue a chance to advance toward the gate where the remaining three men were backing up and firing the remaining bullets from their pistols, desperately trying to reload while the Blue horde closed in on them. There were grins on some members of the Blue as they advanced.

And then…grins on Vidar's men?

Vidar's men dove for cover, clearing the entrance of the gate.

The advancing Blue froze in confusion just as they'd done following the explosions.

A low rumble, and then a deafening roar as an armored roadship plowed through the remnants of the once-fortified gate—plowed through the remnants *and* all Blue members in its way.

Behind the roadship was a screaming charge as more of Vidar's men emerged, rushing through the gate. No pistols that needed concealing upon initial entry for these men—their automatic rifles tore through blue cloth and flesh at will, sending all Blue members scattering in a desperate frenzy.

It was simply a matter of time until the courtyard was cleared, or more appropriately, littered—all things blue and dead the trash.

And so Sadie, who'd been tucked away behind a utility shed in the far east corner of the courtyard, guzzling down the vial of elixir Rafa had fashioned for her so she could expedite healing after utilizing her gift (it wasn't terrible, but she did feel a degree of weakness and nausea), pulled her pistol, tucked her head, and snaked her way through the billowing smoke and mounds of fire, toward the interior of the compound where the remaining members of the Blue had fled.

She wondered whether Vidar, Finn, and Vidar's men were inside already. Had made it through the hatch and were dispatching all Blue members who stood in their path as they ascended towards Gash. She'd given them the station of all Blue members within. Likely, many dispersed after the explosions, either to run out and help, or to run and hide (these were not soldiers like Vidar's men, after all, the majority of them cowards deep down whose courage only came from sheer numbers). Those who *did* run outside to help were greeted with quite the surprise once the armored roadship barreled through, a mass of Vidar's men behind it. If they didn't die from fear after witnessing such a calculated attack, then Vidar's men assuredly put them in the ground seconds after. But those who had not scattered, those who stood their ground inside the compound would be no match for Vidar, Finn, and Vidar's men after they'd emerged from below.

That left Gash and Wrath high above. Sadie had given Vidar the precise location of Gash's nest, the precise blueprint of its layout when she spoke into his soldier's leg minutes ago when she appeared to be pleading. All Vidar and Finn had to do was carry on further up and claim their vengeance. She only wondered whether Gash and Wrath would stick around to fight, or run like—

Sadie dropped to her knees. Pain in her head like she hadn't known in some time came at her like a thousand hangovers, her gift slapping her with something dreadfully new. How had she missed it?

Because you only had five minutes to look, her ego justified through the pain. *Enough time to relay the positions of the Blue standing guard inside, and enough time for the blueprints of Gash's quarters. And that's all. You spotted it, though. It just didn't register until now.*

And before? When I got into Koty's head? How did I miss it then?

You were in there for all of three seconds before you bailed. Or maybe it wasn't even there at the time. But does any of this bullshit hindsight matter? It's there now, and you need to warn them.

Clutching her head as though physically wounded, Sadie struggled to her feet and began unbuttoning her pants, digging inside her pant leg where her own military radio was stitched, the radios Vidar had issued to all in case they needed to give the signal to blow the tunnel.

Sadie would not be signaling to blow the tunnel. But she would be contacting Vidar and Finn and telling them someplace else was wired to blow. Someplace they were likely ascending toward by the second.

forty-five

Entry through the hatch from the tunnel below went seamlessly. One by one they snuck inside the Blue compound unnoticed amongst the chaos. Some members of the Blue even ran by them, paying them no mind as their own frantic need for self-preservation made them blind to any subterfuge.

And that was just fine by Finn. Let Vidar's men handle these scrambling idiots. Or better yet, let them run and *keep on* running as Sadie had predicted they might. What had she said? Moths to a flame? Put out the flame and the moths scatter aimlessly?

Except they hadn't truly put out the flame just yet. Blew on it with a gust hard enough to raise pulses, yes, but the flame still burned; Gash was still alive. And he'd bet the man shielding that flame, preventing it from going out, was still alive too. The man with a penchant for teeth around his neck, the sick freak.

Finn drew his favorite blade. Whistled over toward Vidar, who was in the throes of combat alongside his men. Although "combat" was the wrong descriptor. Combat could indicate a mutual exchange of warfare. This was not the case. "Slaughter" was far more apt.

Vidar and his men tore through any members of the Blue in their way like men battling children, Vidar himself often handling two, three at a time. Finn marveled at his fury. He'd heard the stories, carried out several jobs on his behalf, and formed a friendship of sorts with the man,

but had never actually seen him in battle. It was both awesome and terrifying…and a liability; Finn stood in awe by the stairwell as he watched,
paying his own safety no heed. Vidar taking one member of the Blue by
the neck for a human shield, taking the head clean off the advancing man
to his left with one swipe of his sword, then shoving the human shield
into a man advancing on his right, the two men colliding, Vidar pouncing
on them a second later, grabbing each by the scalp and smashing their
heads together with devastating force, cracking their skulls and killing
them instantly.

And the grin. Vidar was grinning the entire time. Awesome and terrifying. Killing three men in seconds was awesome. The grin throughout
terrifying. For the umpteenth time, Finn was grateful he was on the man's
side.

Finn tried whistling again.

Vidar, having just snapped the neck of a Blue and tossing his limp
body aside effortlessly, heard Finn's call this time. He looked up at Finn
with wild eyes. *What else could be so important?* those wild eyes asked.

Finn pointed towards the ceiling, his gesture indicating that Gash
and Wrath hiding out above was far more important, Vidar, sir.

Vidar nodded once, stepped over the bodies that were accumulat-
ing by the minute at the hands of Vidar's men, and joined Finn by the
stairwell.

Time for the main event, Finn mused. They headed up the stairwell
toward Gash's quarters.

forty-six

"*Come on!*" Sadie screamed. Pants unbuttoned, hand snaked down the length of her leg, she dug frantically to release the radio stitched within its cloth. It would not come free. The angle was too cumbersome, her grip too awkward.

"Screw it," she said and flopped to the ground, kicking up a small cloud of dust as she pulled and wormed her way out of her pants. Finished, she stood in her underwear and fumbled with her pants, eventually finding the leg that held the radio and ripping it free. She brought the radio to her mouth, but got no further.

"What the hell is *this*?" A Blue member, apparently finding refuge in the east corner of the compound by the utility shed as well, approached Sadie with a lecherous grin. "I know I should be going but..." He wrung both hands together like a hungry man about to dig into a meal. "This is just too good to pass up."

Sadie rolled her eyes, placed the radio under her chin to free up both hands, and located the small blade stitched into the lining of the other pant leg. She pulled the blade free and flung it at the advancing Blue member, catching him in the neck and dropping him instantly. The man gurgled on his back, then died.

Sadie immediately went back to the radio. Clicked a switch, pushed a button, and brought the radio to her mouth. "*Hello? Hello? Anyone! Finn?*

Vidar? The nest! Gash's nest above! It's wired to blow! It's wired to blow! *Do not—DO NOT—proceed upwards towards Gash's nest! Hello?!"*

"Sadie?" It was Vidar.

"Vidar! Did you get what I just said? Did it come through?"

"Sadie?"

Sadie cursed, took her thumb off the radio's button, and then pressed it again, harder. *"Vidar, are you there?!"*

Nothing now.

What to do? What to do? Transmission was patchy. A signal. Get them a signal. She looked helplessly at the radio. *What damn signal? We had no prearranged signal for something like this. Only the signal to—*

"VIDAR!" she screamed desperately into the radio.

"Sadie? You there?"

Thank you, thank you. "Do you want me to give the signal to blow the tunnel?!" she asked.

"What?!"

"DO YOU WANT ME TO GIVE THE SIGNAL TO BLOW THE TUNNEL?!"

"What for?!"

"I've been trying to tell you! Gash's nest is wired to—"

forty-seven

The stairs ascending towards Gash's chamber were not a straight shot. They leveled off periodically, branching out into various other dwellings within the rise of the compound.

Finn and Vidar were roughly halfway to the top, now stopping at one of those levels to take cover and listen to Sadie's call.

Vidar cursed at his radio. Turned to Finn and asked: "You get any of that?"

Finn shook his head.

Vidar held the radio to his mouth. "Sadie?"

More static. Vidar cursed again. "Damn things have worked through sandstorms and they choose *now* to be touchy?" He tried again. "Sadie?"

More static.

Vidar looked at the radio in his massive hand as though he meant to crush it. "Piece of shi—"

"*VIDAR!!!*"

Both Vidar and Finn flinched as the radio crackled with Sadie's shout. Vidar replied: "Sadie? You there?"

"*Do you want me to give the signal to blow the tunnel?!*" she asked.

Vidar gave a confused frown. "*What?!*"

"*DO YOU WANT ME TO GIVE THE SIGNAL TO BLOW THE TUNNEL?!*"

Now Vidar and Finn shared a confused frown. Vidar replied: "*What for?!*"

Static again.

Finn asked: "Why the hell would she ask to blow the tunnel?"

Vidar shushed Finn with a hand and went to respond when the entire compound above them exploded, pitching them into blackness.

forty-eight

Finn woke with a boot on his chest and a pistol pointed down at his face. Wrath loomed over him, front teeth as gone as ever, necklace of teeth dangling around his neck fuller than ever. *But he'd make room for mine*, Finn thought. *Oh, yes, he would.*

Wrath removed his boot from Finn's chest and squatted next to him, pressing the barrel of the gun hard into Finn's temple. "You and your ape-friend Vidar did a number on us, Finn, old buddy," he said. "Shame it won't play out to the end."

Not daring to move his head, Finn's eyes strained left, then right, in search of Vidar. He spotted nothing. Nothing at all, in fact. No rubble from the blast. No smoke, no fire, no bodies from the assault below. Where the hell were they?

"A private room, you might say," Wrath said as though reading Finn's mind. "I dragged you in here after the blast." He grinned. "I come here for personal matters."

"Masturbation?" Finn said.

"Funny." He dug the tip of the barrel harder into Finn's temple. "This room…" He gave what amounted to a somewhat nostalgic look around. "You might say I've taken more lives in this room than I can count."

"More than three, was it?"

Wrath offered a lipless smile and shook his head. "Always with the jokes—even in the face of death."

"You're gonna *shoot* me?" Finn asked.

"The thought had occurred to me, but…" Wrath stood again and placed his boot back on Finn's chest. He tossed the gun away, the weapon hitting the stone floor with a dull clatter. He then drew a massive blade from his waist, keeping the pressure of his boot on Finn's chest firm. "Cutting into your flesh will be far more intimate."

Finn pulled a face. "*Intimate?*"

"Oh yes," Wrath breathed.

Finn whipped his forearm into the back of Wrath's leg like a club, buckling his knee and relieving the pressure on his chest. He then rolled to his right, snatched the discarded gun, and scrambled to his feet, gun on Wrath.

Wrath splayed his arms, knife still gripped in his hand. He smirked and threw Finn's own words back at him: "You gonna *shoot* me?"

"Yep." Finn fired two quick shots into Wrath's chest. Wrath flew backwards, dropping his knife, hitting the unforgiving stone floor with a hollow thud.

Finn slowly approached. Wrath lay on his back, labored breaths periodically misting blood into the air, spackling his face as it fell. Now it was Finn who placed his boot on Wrath's chest, the strongest mist of red yet immediately following.

Wrath tried to gurgle something to Finn but managed nothing.

Finn shook his head. "Idiot." He then bent and ripped the necklace of teeth from Wrath's neck. Wrath tried crying out in protest but again managed nothing but a series of red coughs and sputters.

Finn tossed the necklace, spit in Wrath's face, and then shot him between the eyes.

forty-nine

The blast had thrown Vidar from the second level of the compound and into the stairwell, where he tumbled all the way to the bottom, the last several steps unconscious. In addition to this, a sizeable chunk of concrete debris from the blast pinned his leg to the floor, and even someone of Vidar's great strength could not budge it.

Gash couldn't have been more delighted.

Awake now, growling and grunting as he strained every muscle in his body to remove the concrete slab across his leg, Vidar appeared beside himself with rage.

Gash was the opposite. Despite the chaos still brewing outside in the courtyard, his men no match for Vidar's as they inched closer towards the inner sanctum of the Blue compound, Gash remained composed. Standing over Vidar's writhing body, he raised one of the military radios he'd acquired off one of Vidar's fallen men.

"'Blow the tunnel,' huh?" he said. "That *is* what the martyr was screaming to you, yes? I heard every word. And for the life of me, I didn't have a clue as to what she was referring to. But I do now. Oh, yes—you see, after the confusion of the explosion, while you were napping beneath your stone blanket here and Wrath was finishing off your friend Finn, my men and I located the hatch, the entrance to the tunnel. Imagine my surprise. Beneath me all this time." Gash grinned. "How ironic to think that after all this time, your master plan for vengeance will end up becoming my salvation. I certainly can't escape through the main gate. It won't be long now until your men take the courtyard. I'm not so arrogant as to think they won't have me pinned down before long. But this tunnel. This blessed tunnel from which you and your men emerged will see me and my men fleeing…with your body in our wake, of course."

Vidar stopped struggling. "You've been down there already?" he asked.

"My men are down there now as we speak, clearing a secured path for their general."

Vidar said nothing.

Gash turned, bent, and picked up a sizeable chunk of stone, its weight causing him to grunt. "You might think it pains me to have to kill you so quickly," he said. "It does not. *You* were always the one with the vendetta, Vidar, not me. And I understand your hate. What I did to your family…" He grinned again. "You did come so very close; I'll give you that."

Gash raised the stone overhead. "Must be going now. Your tunnel awaits me."

fifty

Izar and Teir stood firm amongst Vidar's men by the tunnel entrance, Izar periodically stroking the enormous Gatling gun as though it were a horse.

The voices they'd heard in the distance, at first hard to distinguish if echoing from above or encroaching, were growing stronger now. All of them male.

It wasn't right.

Izar strapped herself in behind the Gatling gun.

Vidar's men readied their weapons.

"*Hold…*" Vidar's primary man in charge whispered. "*Keep radio silence. If these are our men, they would have told us by now.*"

The echoing voices growing closer.

"*Hold…*"

The faintest of many silhouettes now suddenly appearing in the distant black.

"*Light 'em up.*"

In retrospect, she would feel periodic bouts of guilt, but at the time, Izar had the time of her life laying every one of them to waste.

fifty-one

A member of the Blue, bloodied and desperate, stumbled onto the scene just as Gash was about to bring the stone down onto Vidar's head.

"*A trap!*" the man screamed, clutching his abdomen. Blood poured from what appeared to be multiple wounds.

Gash froze, stone above his head. "*What?!*"

"*The tunnel is no exit!!! It's filled with—*" Two simultaneous bullets stopped his cries cold: one to the head, and a second to the chest. The man crumpled and died instantly.

Both Finn and Sadie emerged, Sadie from the east, Finn from the stairwell. The pistols they'd used on the gang member were now on Gash.

Vidar smiled.

Gash steadied his grip on the stone, positioned it directly over Vidar's head. "Shoot me and he's dead," he said.

"Shoot him," Vidar said.

"*Any* shot that hits me will cause a reflex to let go. His skull will split wide open," Gash said through gritted teeth.

"Shoot him," Vidar said again.

"Put down your guns," Gash told Sadie and Finn.

"Vidar's men are going to be storming in here any minute, Gash," Sadie said. "Trust me; I just came from outside. Your men didn't stand a chance." The sounds of gunfire and pain echoed in from the courtyard as if to underline Sadie's words.

"And the same will apply to them!" Gash said. "They shoot, and their general dies. Now put down your guns and kick them over here. This stone is heavy, and I'm eager to let go."

Vidar struggled furiously against the stone slab on his leg.

"He's not going anywhere, and my arms grow weary," Gash said.

"Sadie. Finn. If you kick your guns over to him, and I survive this, I'm going to shoot you myself," Vidar said.

"*DO IT!*" Gash yelled.

Sadie and Finn exchanged a glance.

"*NOW!*"

They slid their guns over.

Gash then gestured to Sadie with his chin. "*You*—over here."

Sadie approached.

"Here—next to me," Gash said.

Again Sadie reluctantly obeyed.

Gash suddenly heaved the stone in Finn's direction, then spun and drove his fist into Sadie's gut, dropping her to both knees. He then bent and snatched one of the discarded guns and yanked Sadie back to her feet, wrapping his forearm around her throat and pressing the gun to her head. Sadie struggled to breathe from both the blow and Gash's grip.

"Now, this is what I like to call a bit of leverage," Gash said with a smile as he began dragging Sadie backwards towards the hatch's location. "Might I suggest you radio down there and let them know we're coming? Would be a shame if they shot us both."

Finn, jaw clenched until the muscles on either side bulged like knots, drew his radio. "It's Finn," he managed. "Come back."

The radio crackled, then responded. "*Finn? We just had a bunch of—*"

"Yeah, I know. Listen to me. Two more are headed down."

"*Let them come. We'll be ready.*"

"No you *won't*. One of them will be Sadie."

"*Okay, no problem. We'll stand down. Who's the other?*"

Finn grimaced as though in deep physical pain. "Gash."

"*What?!*"

"Don't make me say it again," Finn said. "Just stand down on anyone approaching. Gash has the upper hand."

"Well said, Finn," Gash said as he continued backing away toward the hatch with a firm grip on Sadie. Nearly out of sight now, Gash pulled Sadie in tighter. "What do you say, honey? Shall we get going?" He licked Sadie's cheek, a long vile drag with his thick tongue.

Sadie winced as though his tongue were a blade.

"You're not gonna win, you piece of shit," Finn said. "Your men are all but finished. I killed Wrath stone dead. You've got *nothing*."

"On the contrary," Gash said. "I've got her—" He squeezed Sadie tight. "A martyr's gift is all I need to get back on my feet. And though I prefer them younger, I will definitely make do with this one's beauty." He went to lick her again but Sadie managed to turn her head and avoid most of it.

The sound of gunfire outside was becoming more sporadic. Vidar's men were closing in.

"Must be going now," Gash said. He glanced down towards Vidar. Curiously quiet throughout the last few exchanges, Vidar had been working on the stone slab again with insane intensity, his skin purple with effort, thick veins bulging and zig-zagging on every available muscle. Still the slab was going nowhere.

"Maybe in the next life, Vidar," Gash said. Then up at Finn: "As for your life—" Gash shot Finn in the chest.

Finn flew back into the stairwell.

Sadie cried out.

Gash grinned, placed the gun back to Sadie's head, and then dragged her away.

fifty-two

Vidar's head man lowered the radio and looked at his surrounding team in disbelief.

"Gash is coming down with *Sadie*?" Teir said.

Vidar's man nodded, visibly upset.

"*Why?*" Izar asked.

Vidar's man shook his head. "I imagine the reasons are not good."

"So what do we do?" Izar asked.

"We do as we're told," he said. "We stand down."

Izar worked her way out from behind the Gatling gun and approached Vidar's head man. "And let that animal into our community? With Sadie?"

"That's right," he said. "You heard Finn. Gash has the upper hand."

"We could still blow the tunnel," one of Vidar's soldiers suggested.

"*What about Sadie?*" Teir blurted.

The soldier did not look at Teir, but at Vidar's head man, when he replied: "We'd get Gash."

"*No!*" Teir yelled.

Vidar's head man looked away in thought as though considering it.

"You can't be serious," Izar said. "After all Sadie has done for us…"

His gaze broke. "This is war, Izar. There are casualties of war. Some greater than others in order to ensure victory."

"Oh yeah? Why don't you radio on up to Finn again? Ask *him* what he thinks about this stupid idea? Go on; do it!"

Vidar's man took a deep breath, sighed, and brought the radio to his chin. "Finn? Finn, come back."

Nothing.

"Finn? Finn, you there? Come back."

Still nothing.

Izar grabbed the radio from him. "Finn? Finn, it's Izar? They want to blow the tunnel! They want to blow the tunnel and kill them *both*—Gash *and* Sadie! Finn…? *Finn…?*"

Vidar's head man took the radio back from Izar.

"Something must be wrong," Izar said.

"Or maybe he can't bring himself to answer what he knows is the right thing to do," he said.

"No!" Izar cried out again. "We can't do this! We—"

Teir bolted into the tunnel.

"*TEIR!*"

Vidar's head man lunged for him and missed. He made an effort at a few paces in before backing out. "It's black as night in there, dammit—" He glanced back towards the tunnel. "He'll be blind."

Izar thought: *No, he won't.*

fifty-three

Gash continued dragging Sadie backwards as he worked his way through the tunnel. Sadie wriggled and wormed, not in a bid to escape, but to alleviate the pressure around her neck.

"So, where are we headed, beautiful?" Gash asked her. "What's waiting at the other end of the tunnel?"

"Many bullets in your tiny brain."

Gash laughed. "Really? Your friends would risk killing you in an effort to get to me?"

"Yes."

"I doubt that. The dearly departed Finn did not hesitate in putting down his weapon to save your life. Why would his men be any bolder?"

"They aren't Finn's men, you idiot; they're Vidar's. Vidar would put a bullet in my chest if he could be sure it would come out the other side and hit you."

Gash laughed again, continued dragging Sadie through the black of the tunnel, his grip on her neck unyielding.

Sadie considered her words. *Would* Vidar do such a thing? He was pinned beneath that debris the whole time, struggling like mad to get free. Suppose it was the other way around? Suppose Finn was pinned down and Vidar was the one holding the gun on Gash and her. Would he have relinquished his weapon? Or would he have done exactly as she so brazenly claimed and shot *through* her if it meant getting to Gash?

Why not? she thought. *That's what I'd do.*

(*No, you wouldn't. You* would *have, but not anymore. Things are different now.*)

Bullshit.

(*Your life has purpose now.*)

Big heaping mound of bullshit.

(*You know it's true.*)

Even if it is, it's irrelevant now, isn't it?

"*If you can find his butt…*"

What???

"*If you can find his ear…*"

What the hell is—?

"*…find his hips…*"

KIDDO? Is that you???

"*I got this.*"

"You're quiet, girl," Gash said. "Using your freak gift, are you? Trying to see if, forgive me, there *is* light at the end of the tunnel for you?" He barked out a solitary laugh at his own pun…only to jerk suddenly and say: "What the hell was that? Did you just touch my ass—*AAAAAAAHHHHH!!!*"

Gash released his hold on Sadie and dropped to one knee, gun hitting the tunnel floor with a clatter as he clutched the back of his leg in agony.

Unseeing hands found Gash's ears next, each thumb on those hands locating and going for the eyes. Though Gash's one eye was long dead, it was still susceptible to pain, as was assuredly the case with the other. He cried out again and brought both hands up, knocking the burrowing thumbs away and rubbing furiously at both eyes…

…leaving his waist exposed.

"*You can find his hips, you can find his twig and berries…Knife 'em, strike 'em, or squeeze 'em for all you're worth. Up to you. They're all a good time.*"

Teir once again unsheathed the blade he'd used on Gash's hamstring.

Sadie sensed it coming, reached down, and found Teir's wrist, stopping him. "Save some for your grandfather, kiddo."

Teir's arm relaxed in Sadie's grip. Sadie took the knife from him. And Teir settled for kicking Gash square in the balls.

fifty-four

Vidar's men eventually broke through, entering the compound to find their general pinned beneath an enormous slab of stone, and Finn nursing a gunshot that had just missed his heart, hitting his upper left shoulder instead.

"*Get this damn thing off of me!*" Vidar screamed.

Vidar's men rushed to his aid and eventually heaved the slab off their general's leg. The underlying result was not good. The leg was a shattered mess. But this did not stop Vidar from dragging himself to his feet and hobbling towards the courtyard. Two of his men immediately flanked him for human crutches.

Finn, keeping firm pressure on his wound with a stained-red shred of clothing from a dead gang member, stood and followed close behind. "*Where are you going?*"

"To my grandson. We need to enter his community from their primary entrance before Gash makes his way through that tunnel."

"Vidar, that's *miles* away," Finn said.

"We have a roadship," he replied. Then, to his men who were not acting as his crutches: "Go ready it for exit."

His men immediately obeyed and headed out towards the smoldering aftermath within the courtyard.

"And what will you do when you reach the community's primary entrance?" Finn asked.

Vidar ignored him, nudging his men to help him onward, out into the courtyard.

"Vidar, he has Sadie. We need to think this through."

Vidar spun, his size nearly flinging both men supporting him aside. *"What would you have me do?!"*

Finn, to his own surprise, hollered back. "I don't know! But arriving there before Gash can make his escape won't change the fact that he still has Sadie as leverage!"

Vidar and Finn stared hard at one another, both nearly panting with adrenaline and pain.

A radio buzzed on one of Vidar's men. "Finn? Vidar? It's the tunnel. Come back."

Vidar's man went to respond, but Vidar snatched the radio from him before he could. "This is Vidar. Come back."

"We've got him, General."

Vidar and Finn exchanged a look.

"Come again?" Vidar said.

"We've got Gash."

Vidar frowned, shook his head. "I don't—*how's that?*"

"You can thank your grandson, General. He all but did it single-handedly."

"The blind kid?" Finn blurted.

Vidar shot him a look. Finn gave an apologetic nod.

"My grandson?" Vidar said. "How?"

"Get on down here. I'm sure he'll be proud to tell you himself."

Vidar paused a moment, then raised the radio again. "Is he still alive?" he asked. "Gash, I mean."

"Yes, sir, he is."

Vidar's smirk that followed scared even Finn.

"Excellent," he said. "We're on our way."

fifty-five

Seven months later...

The riddle was spoken through the door in an undertone, as if a lack of volume might increase its opacity.

"Nine times horizon five."

Rafa provided the answer without so much as a pause.

"Zero."

The riddles were a necessary layer of security, this he well understood. They simply did not perplex him as they did other people. At first, the ease with which he deduced the answers had embarrassed him, and he had pretended to struggle before giving them. Now, after so many visits over the past seven months, he no longer feigned struggle in the least. In fact, Rafa had grown quite comfortable with the ritual of gaining entry to the inner sanctum of Vidar's fortress. This was due in no small part to Vidar's relentlessly effusive appreciation for Rafa's intelligence.

A burst of deep laughter followed by a chorus of barking dogs echoed from behind the guard who opened the heavy door. The sound of music—a recording of a violin concerto—accompanied the cacophony.

"Rafael!" Vidar shouted as he rose from his armchair. "Enter!" The big man limped across the room, leaning heavily on his cane, a trio of large, rambunctious young dogs at his heels, and embraced Rafa. "How are you, my boy?"

"Very well, sir. And you?"

"Very well. Very well indeed. My ego has nearly recovered from our chess match last week. I've some lingering humiliation, but I'm ready to face you again if you'll indulge me at some point in the near future."

Rafa smiled. "Of course."

"Excellent! You're staying the night, correct?"

"Yes, if that's all right. I'm sorry I'm late. I came alone on Sadie's motorhorse. I'd rather not ride all the way back tonight."

Vidar placed a huge hand on Rafa's shoulder and squeezed as he focused an unusually solemn stare into Rafa's eyes. "It is my *honor* to host you, son. You know that." Then he turned to the guard who had admitted Rafa into the room. "Pour Dr. Carrera Allende and me a pair of whiskeys."

The guard nodded silently and headed for the bar in the corner.

"Come, let us get comfortable," Vidar said. "Dinner's in an hour."

Rafa followed him and the dogs to the well-appointed seating area. The big man eased himself back into his armchair, and the dogs began a three-way wrestling match nearby.

Koty rose from the huge leather couch, hugged Rafa tightly, and kissed his cheek.

On the couch behind Koty sat Teir, a broad smile on his face and a sleeping infant sprawled against his chest. "You're late," Teir admonished him playfully. "Took the long way flying solo on Sadie's motorhorse again?"

Rafa felt his windswept face warm. "Is it that obvious?"

"Even to my eyes."

Vidar unleashed another rumble of laughter at his grandson's joke as one of the dogs began barking in mock ferocity at the other two. Rafa marveled at how the tiny girl in Teir's arms slept so soundly.

Koty gave voice to his thoughts. "I still have no idea how she sleeps through all this noise while at home in our quiet little apartment she wakes at the slightest sound."

"She must feel very comfortable here," Rafa said. "Perhaps our community is too quiet for her."

Koty raised an eyebrow at him and chuckled, a bittersweet response that spoke volumes. The irony in his explanation was clearly not lost on her. "If that's true, then too bad for her," she said, "because as much as I enjoy visiting here, I love our home." She gave Teir's boot an affectionate tap with her own. "Fortunately, she feels comfortable in Teir's arms no matter where she is."

Keeping a protective hand on the child's back, Teir reached up to take Koty's hand and tug her gently down to sit beside him, his arm draped across her shoulders. "I love our home too." He kissed her cheek. "And there's enough of me for both of you."

The guard returned bearing a silver tray with two whiskeys. Rafa took a glass and seated himself in the empty chair beside Vidar's.

The big man raised his glass to Rafa. "Here's to me getting you drunk enough to lose a game of chess."

Rafa laughed and raised his own glass in salute, then drank.

． ． ．

Sadie inhaled deeply, filling her lungs with the cool desert night air as it poured in through the open windows of the roadship. One hand on the wheel, she stuck the other out the window and let the wind hit her open palm, felt it rush through her fingers. Her foot pressed the accelerator a little more. The engine roared, and the roadship surged forward as if a giant hand had just given them a shove.

"You're not going to let me drive at all, are you?" Finn asked from the passenger seat.

"Nope. I'm having way too much fun."

Finn just chuckled and shook his head. "Are you at least going to tell me where we're going?"

"Do we need to have an immediate destination? As long as we're at Vidar's tomorrow afternoon to bring Kiddo and his little ladies back to the community, who cares where the night takes us? We've got plenty of fuel. Let's just drive."

She felt Finn staring at her in the darkness. Then she reached a little with her gift and felt a swirl of his thoughts: Irritation. Confusion. Amusement. Curiosity. Exhilaration.

His words attempted a droll disguise. "Meaning you drive while I ride along."

"That sounds about right."

Another chuckle and shake of the head from him.

"You wanna stop for a drink somewhere?" she asked. "Maybe a few hands of cards?"

"*Cards*? Are you serious?"

She grinned. "I'm feeling lucky."

about the authors

jeff menapace

A native of the Philadelphia area, Jeff has published multiple works in both fiction and non-fiction. In 2011 he was the recipient of the Red Adept Reviews Indie Award for Horror.

Jeff's terrifying debut novel *Bad Games* became a #1 Kindle bestseller that spawned two acclaimed sequels, and now all three books in the trilogy have been optioned for feature films and translated for foreign audiences.

His other novels, along with his award-winning short works, have also received international acclaim and are eagerly waiting to give you plenty of sleepless nights.

Free time for Jeff is spent watching horror movies, The Three Stooges, and mixed martial arts. He loves steak and more steak, thinks the original 1974 *Texas Chainsaw Massacre* is the greatest movie ever, wants to pet a lion someday, and hates spiders.

He currently lives in Pennsylvania with his wife Kelly and their cats Sammy and Bear.

Jeff loves to hear from his readers. Please feel free to contact him to discuss anything and everything, and be sure to visit his website to sign up for his FREE newsletter (no spam, not ever) where you will receive updates and sneak peeks on all future works along with the occasional free goodie!

connect with jeff on facebook, twitter, linkedin, goodreads, and instagram

www.facebook.com/JeffMenapace.writer
http://twitter.com/JeffMenapace
https://www.linkedin.com/in/jeffmenapace
https://www.goodreads.com/jeffmenapace
https://www.instagram.com/jeffmenapace

other works by jeff menapace

Please visit Jeff's Amazon Author Page or his website for a complete list of all available works!
http://www.amazon.com/Jeff-Menapace/e/B004R09M0S
www.jeffmenapace.com

kim bravo

Kim Bravo lives in Philadelphia, PA with her husband Rodrigo and a few freeloading cats.

authors' note

Thank you so much for taking the time to read *Cling*. Kim and I hope you enjoyed reading about our crazy world of martyrs and moles as much as we did creating it.

If we succeeded in entertaining you, Kim and I would be very grateful if you took a few minutes to write a review on Amazon for *Cling*. Good reviews are always helpful, and we would absolutely love to read the various insights from satisfied readers.

Thank you so very much. Until Sadie cheats at Powerball…

Jeff Menapace
Kim Bravo

CPSIA information can be obtained
at www.ICGtesting.com
Printed in the USA
LVHW041702040419
612996LV00004B/645